Selkie Moon

Kelly Jarvis

INCANTATION PRESS

Orkney
Scotland
FAIR ISLE CHANNEL
TO SHETLAND
ATLANTIC OCEAN
Papa Westray
North Ronaldsay
Westray
Sanday
Eday
Rousay
Egilsay
Stronsay
Wyre
Gairsay
Mainland Orkney
Shapinsay
KIRKWALL
NORTH SEA
Hoy
Burray
South Ronaldsay
PENTLAND FIRTH
Mainland Scotland

"A soft breeze stirs and all my thoughts are blown
Far out to sea and lost"
(Edwin Muir)

One

The Orkney Islands, the lands that I call home, float in the frigid waters where the North Sea kisses the Atlantic, between Scotland and the Shetland Islands, beneath a multitude of skies.

In winter months, our bright blue skies shimmer for just a few short hours before brilliant day is swept away by the inky cloth of night, and on the solstice in midsummer, which we call the simmer dim, our dusty twilight skies linger long after the islands' housekeepers have packed away their brooms and gone to bed. Our morning skies usher in banks of faraway clouds, our evening skies paint the ocean's froth with the crimson hues of sunset, and, most beautiful of all, our full moon skies shimmer like silver coins tossed across beds of thick, black velvet.

My father told me I was born beneath a full moon sky that coated the coastline with dancing, diamond light. "You slid down from heaven on a moonbeam," he used to say each time he told me the story of my birth, "and when the angels saw how beautiful you looked nestled in your mother's arms, they tore out the feathers of their wings in anger over the loss of you."

He would tuck me into bed as he described the fierce storm that followed my arrival, and I would burrow beneath my covers, protecting myself from the winds and rains of my imagination as he spoke. "The ocean tides were so strong that your mother and I worried our island might be torn in two," he would say, his voice deep and resonant as his hands moved through the air, evoking the rush and swell of invading water. He would cup my chin in his calloused fingers and look directly into my eyes, delivering the final lines of his bedtime story with practiced precision. "Your mother and I didn't need to worry. Our island may be small, but it is strong enough to weather any storm."

He would dim the light and step into the hallway, leaving me to fall asleep on my own, but not before reminding me why he had named me after the islands that sheltered us and gave us safe harbor. "Always remember, Isla, you are as strong and as constant as the land beneath your feet." I was only a little girl, and I didn't feel very strong, but I would nod my head in agreement to make my father smile.

My father, a farmer and a fisherman, was woven into the fabric of Orkney life, his family spread like freckles across the broad face of the islands. He had been born and raised on Mainland, the largest and most populated island in the archipelago, separated from the northern coast of Scotland by the tumultuous Pentland Firth. Although my father took me to visit my grandparents' and uncles' houses on Mainland during

Kelly Jarvis

the holiday season, we spent the majority of my early years on the shores of North Ronaldsay, the remote island where my father first met my mother, and fell hopelessly in love.

My mother, silent and solitary, was the wild night to my father's distinguished day. She rarely accompanied us to Mainland when we travelled, claiming she could not forgo her household duties to make the journey, and, when old Mrs. Tulloch volunteered to watch me on Saturday nights so that my mother could join my father and his friends at the crowded tavern in the center of town, she always made an excuse. My mother preferred to stay home with me, staring out the window at the wide expanse of the Atlantic Ocean while I entertained myself with my puzzles and dolls.

Throughout my childhood, I watched my parents' strange love story unfold, piecing its mysteries together from my own observations and my father's tall tales. "Have I ever told you about the first time I was caught in a tempest at sea?" my father asked me one night after he and my mother had had one of their vicious rows. I had been awakened from sleep by the loud sounds of overturned chairs and shattering porcelain, and when I crept from my room and saw my mother running toward the beach, I cried out to her and tried to follow. My father caught me in his arms and carried me back into the house, holding me against his chest until I stopped kicking and screaming.

"I thought the storm would last forever, Isla." His words were steady against my sobs. He dried my tears with the sleeve of his shirt. "But the storm always ends," he said. "The sea always calms. The sun always rises again."

I didn't understand why he was talking about the sea instead of chasing my mother into the night so that he could bring her back home to us. The rocks outside our cottage were slick with salt spray, and I was afraid she might slip and fall into the deep, dark water. I was tired and scared, and I wanted my mother to sing to me and comfort me like she had when I was a baby. I began to cry again, and a look of impatience clouded my father's face.

He set me down on the floor and lifted a glass to his lips, swallowing the dregs of amber liquid still clinging to the bottom. He closed his eyes and let out a deep sigh.

"Go to bed, Isla," he commanded.

"But—"

"Your mother will be home soon." He poured more of the bitter-smelling liquid into his glass and tipped his head back to let the whisky slide down his throat. "She'll never leave us," he reassured me, placing the glass back down on the table. "She'll never leave you."

"But—"

"Go to bed, Isla," he repeated, his voice stern and final.

When I woke the next morning, my mother was at the stove frying kippers and oatcakes for my breakfast. My father stood behind her, running his hands through the strands of her long, loose hair. She made a sound, deep and guttural, as he caressed the back of her neck. Then he turned her around and kissed her, locking her tight in his embrace.

I watched them, but if my parents noticed my presence, they made no move to acknowledge me. They looked only

Kelly Jarvis

at each other, whispering words I could not hear as my breakfast sizzled and burned in the pan.

It wasn't until I was old enough to spend time in the homes of my school friends that I learned my parents' relationship was unsettling. Other couples seemed more suited to one another, moving in unison like the migrating birds that soar overhead and nest among the cliffs each spring. My parents, whose devotion to each other was both timeless and terrifying, churned and swirled in opposite directions, like two enormous oceans that meet with the crashing of salty tears.

For seventeen years, I was the island between them.

Two

North Ronaldsay is a low-lying swath of land surrounded by dangerous waters known as "the graveyard of ships." The island is circled by a drystone dyke designed to protect the cultivated farmlands of the interior from the feral sheep which roam the rocky western shores feasting on seaweed and kelp. Storm surges and rip tides eat away at the dyke, so the men must make constant repairs if they hope to maintain the barrier between the island's wild coast and its civilized center.

We lived in a little house on the eastern side of the island near Linklet Bay where waters lap gently against an arcing sandy shore. When the tide was low, my father would take me to explore the pools of water left behind, clutching my hand so I would not slip as he pointed out signs of teeming life clinging to the rocks and stones. My mother preferred the pounding surf on the island's western shore, and she let me run wild in the crashing waves as she swam and dove at my side. When her mood turned melancholy and she wandered the rocks lost in thought, I searched for playmates in the kind faces of grey seals that bobbed in the ocean swells just beyond my reach.

It was my father who would tuck me in at the end of each day, sending me to sleep with his stories even when the summer sun still hung high above the horizon. Like all fishermen who hone their craft during long days spent between the sea and sky, my father could paint pictures with his words, and he was known as a raucous storyteller at the local pub. He told me of his boyhood experiences on the islands and recited fairy tales from memory, but my favorite stories were the ones he created about the wild sheep who broke into the bakery each night to cook seaweed cakes, or about the enchanted fish who swam in oceans stained purple by rains that fell from ruby-studded skies.

My father's stories always ended with a magic kiss upon my forehead which he said would put even the most wide-awake princess to sleep, but I never slept until I opened the drawer of my wooden nightstand to see what waited inside. I knew I would find a treasure my mother had collected during the day, perhaps a marbled pebble that had washed up on the shore, a piece of driftwood carved by ocean currents, a shard of sea glass worn smooth by the waves, or a limpet shell, its underside glistening in shades of green and periwinkle blue. My mother never spoke to me of these treasures, but I came to think of them as her way of telling me a story, and I would hold each night's secret gift in the hollow of my hand, turning it over and over as I drifted off to sleep.

I often begged my father to tell me stories about my mother, for although I was her constant companion, she was quiet and elusive, a riddle I could never quite solve. "The first time I saw your mother, I was fourteen years old," my father began as I settled against the pillows one winter evening. "My uncle had taken my brothers and I to the Fair Isle Channel to fish for trout and halibut, and we decided to spend the night on North Ronaldsay before heading home to Mainland."

He struck a match against the ceramic surface of my nightstand, letting the flame burn in the air for a few seconds before circling it above the tobacco piled in the bowl of his pipe.

"It was the simmer dim, and the sun and moon both hung in the milky sky," he said, taking several steady puffs. I had always wanted to stay up all night during the simmer dim to watch the daylight win its celestial battle against the dark, but my parents had never allowed it. "I couldn't sleep," my father continued, reading my thoughts as he playfully tugged my hair, "and since I wasn't a good little girl, like you, I snuck outside to walk along the shore."

His pipe glowed fiery red, throwing light and shadow across my bedspread. "She was singing and dancing on the rocks," he said, his eyes growing hazy with the memory. "She was surrounded by a circle of her sisters and cousins. The tide was high, and the waves were slamming against the craggy shore. She laughed as the water splashed over her, and the sound of her laughter made my heart skip a beat."

Although my father was sitting in the chair next to my bed, holding my hand as he spoke, I knew that in his mind,

 Kelly Jarvis

he was walking the shoreline of a long ago summer solstice, watching my mother dance in the perpetual dusk, her soft, brown hair falling in wild ringlets down her back.

"I hid behind a boulder, barely breathing, trying not to disturb their sacred dance," my father continued. "I didn't think anyone could see me, but she turned around and met my gaze. Her eyes were as grey as the skies during a winter gale, and I knew, then and there, that I was going to make her my wife."

"Did you ask her to marry you?"

My small voice pierced his recollection. He turned to look at me, surprise wrinkling his brow, as though he had forgotten I was in the room.

"No," he laughed, shaking his head. "I was too young to get married, and too shy to speak to her." His voice grew quiet, and I leaned closer to hear it. The sweet tobacco-scent of his breath wafted over me. "I didn't see your mother again for another seven years, but her wild grey eyes haunted me. I used to hear her song in the howling of the winds and the rushing of the water when I fished the open ocean." He turned toward the window where a crescent moon sailed through windswept skies. "I still hear her song," he said, "when I spend the night at sea."

I hated it when my father's work kept him away overnight. Our home was quiet without him, and I had heard the sailors' warnings about the dangerous North Sea. I liked thinking that my mother's song might follow my father across the waves, keeping him safe from harm until he returned home to us again.

My father stood up, breaking the spell his story had cast. He tucked my blankets firmly into the gap between my mattresses and kissed me goodnight, ignoring my pleas that he continue his tale. I had a thousand questions about my mother, and a thousand more about the aunts and cousins I had never met, but bedtime had come, and my father would hear none of them.

That night I dreamed of walking along the coast in the nautical twilight of the simmer dim. The surf was running high, and I took shelter behind the rocks, watching a shadowy group of women sing and dance. When they finally turned around to acknowledge me, they had the black wool faces of our feral island sheep, and their ruby-red eyes glowed like fire in the sun.

Kelly Jarvis

Three

My little brother was born in the seventh year of my life beneath a night sky that rippled with green and purple ribbons of northern light. My mother had labored all day, grunting and moaning with increased frequency as she went about her chores. When the evening grew dusky, she packed a small bag with my toys and blankets and took me to the rocky beach where she had first taught me to swim. She told me to stay by the seagrass. Then she walked to the ocean's edge and lowered herself onto the wet sand, letting the cold water wash over her cramping abdomen. The late autumn air was thin and clear, and I watched the stars flicker in the growing darkness, each one a candle in the ebony sky.

It was hours before my father found us. I heard his voice and the pounding of his footsteps on the path long before I saw him. He must have come home after working in the fields and panicked when he realized we were gone.

"Isla!" He dropped to his knees, pulling me up from my seat so that my face was level with his. "Where's your mother?"

I pointed toward the shoreline. My father's eyes followed the direction of my finger. He squinted as he tried to discern my mother's body from the grey rocks that grew out of the heaving sea. As soon as he saw her, waist deep in the swirling waves, he let go of me and ran to her, losing his footing on the slippery pebbles as he struggled against the incoming tide.

I couldn't hear my parents' voices over the wailing winds, but I knew they were fighting with each other. My father tried to pull my mother from the ocean, likely telling her that she needed to go to the medical center in town where Dr. Sutherland, our island's only physician, would supervise the baby's birth. My mother spat at him, shaking her head and pushing him away. I was afraid he was going to force her from the sea against her will, but when her body tightened with a new contraction, he wrapped his arms around her, lowering himself into the water behind her as she trembled in pain.

I must have fallen asleep on the shore and been carried back home, because the next thing I remember was waking up in my parents' bedroom. My mother rested on the bed beside me, holding a blanket-wrapped baby in her arms. She smiled at me and pulled me closer so I could see him.

He was beautiful. He had eyes the color of a rolling grey sea mist, and his tiny body was completely covered by downy white fur. A web of gossamer skin, translucent in the light and as thin as paper, stretched between each of his fingers and toes. He mewled as my mother sang us a lullaby in a foreign tongue that was as familiar to me as the beating of her heart.

"He swam up to us from the bottom of the sea," my father explained as he entered the room and began to spin the story

Kelly Jarvis

of my brother's birth. I laughed and shook my head. I knew the baby had come from inside my mother because I had watched her womb grow round with him.

"What's his name?" I asked, marveling at how small he was.

"His name is Callan," my father answered, "after the rocks that surround our island's coastline."

"Callan," I said.

My mother's eyes flashed at the earthy sound of the baby's name in my mouth. I knew she didn't like it, but I also knew her feelings about it hardly mattered because she would never use it. In the seven years of memories I had accumulated before my brother's birth, I could not remember my mother ever calling me Isla. When she wanted my attention, she would simply click her tongue against the roof of her mouth three times in quick succession. The sound was soft and inviting when I needed comfort, percussive and sharp when I was in trouble.

"Callan," my father repeated, lifting the baby from my mother's chest and looking at him with pride. "My son."

❋

Callan learned to swim in the frigid seas surrounding our island long before he learned to walk. Although my father had forbidden my mother from bringing us to the western shores on her own, he worked long hours every day, and my mother did as she pleased. She would hold the baby against her chest as the three of us floated on the whitecaps, Callan giggling as the waves crashed over him, his laugh a loud and infectious bleat. By spring he had learned to pull himself across the sands with his arms, and as autumn once again darkened our days, he delighted in the early squalls of snow that decorated the roof of our house as though it were a cupcake topped with spun sugar.

One night as my father was putting me to bed, telling me an exciting story about his battles with a colony of fish-stealing seals off the coast of Westray, I let it slip that my mother had disobeyed his command to keep Callan and me out of the western waters.

"If you sing to a seal, it will grant your deepest desire," I had said, confident in my knowledge about seal folklore because I had read about it in one of my books. "You should try singing to the seals off Westray, and then ask them not to steal your fish."

My father laughed, his pipe clicking against his teeth. "Since when can a seal make a wish come true?" he teased.

I sat up, laughing with him, but determined to convince him the old wives' tale was true. "Since this morning," I countered. "Earlier today, I told a grey seal that I wished I had some chocolate biscuits, and then you brought chocolate biscuits home from the bakery." It had been a near-perfect day; after my wished-for dessert had been eaten, my mother and father had danced around the cottage with Callan and me, letting me stay up for an extra hour after the baby had gone to bed.

My father's eyes narrowed. He removed his pipe from his mouth, grasping it in his hand so tightly that his knuckles turned white.

"Where did you see a grey seal?" he asked.

A chill ran down my spine as I realized what I had said. Grey seals, which were almost never seen near Linklet Bay, were common on the western shores of our island.

"I meant a harbor seal," I whispered, trying, but failing, to fix my mistake. A family of harbor seals nested on the shoals in the gentle waters outside our home, and I hoped my father would believe that I had been talking with one of them. "I asked a harbor seal for chocolate biscuits, and then you brought some home from the bakery."

A moment of silence stretched between us before my father spoke again.

"Don't lie to me, Isla," he said. His voice was angry and tight.

I was an avid reader, and the pages of my picture books were filled with detailed illustrations of the birds and beasts found in the skies and waters surrounding Orkney. My father and I both knew I would never confuse a grey seal with a harbor seal.

"Where did you see a grey seal?" he asked again when I tried to look away from him.

My mother had never told me to lie to my father about our excursions to the western shores, but I had always kept our trips a secret. The wild beaches where the feral sheep roamed were special places to us, and I didn't want my father to tell me I was no longer allowed to visit them.

"Isla—"

He spoke my name as though he was issuing a warning. "Don't make me ask you again."

I started to cry, promising him that my mother always kept Callan and me safe when we swam in the rough Atlantic swells, not understanding that my defense of her was simply proof of her refusal to honor his wishes. He stood up and turned down the light.

"Don't leave your room," he said, closing my door behind him.

I hid my face in my pillow as I listened to my parents argue, my father's booming words rising above my mother's unintelligible bark.

"You promised me I could trust you," he yelled.

"I'm their father!"

"I need to know they're safe when I'm away!"

Soon his shouting was replaced by the sounds of a violent struggle and then the loud thump of the closet door hitting the wall as it was pulled open. My father kept his old sea chest at the bottom of our hall closet, and I heard him drag it across the floor, its metal padlock clanging against the heavy oak panels. My father never let me play with his sea chest, and he refused to tell me what he kept locked inside. I wondered why he was taking it out now, but my curiosity dissolved as my mother's cries rent the air. They were not cries of pain or anger; they were cries of despair, and they broke my heart in two. I covered my ears with my hands, but I couldn't block out the sound of her screams or the acrid smell of burning wood drifting down the hall.

Callan woke up, and when he began to wail, my parents abruptly stopped arguing. I heard the front door slam shut, and the orange glow which had flared in the narrow space of

 Kelly Jarvis

light between my carpet and my bedroom door dissolved into a haze of grey smoke.

My father had ordered me to stay in my room, but I slipped from beneath my covers and crept down the hall. I found my mother nursing Callan, something she hadn't done since he was a newborn. Her milk had calmed him, and his webbed fingers twisted the ringlets of her hair in contentment. My father's heavy sea chest lay in the center of the room. The top right corner was charred black. The burned remains of a blanket that had been thrown across the flames stained the floor with ash.

"What happened?" I asked, ashamed that my inability to keep my mother's secrets about our trips to the coast had ruined such a beautiful day. "Where's Papa?"

My mother only shook her head. I was worried she would blame me for my father's anger, but when she clicked her tongue against the roof of her mouth, the sound was forgiving and sweet. I climbed up onto her lap next to Callan and folded myself into the warmth of her body. She kissed the tears from my cheeks and sang to me until I fell asleep.

In my dreams, the notes of her lullaby grew wings, soaring across the ocean like seabirds until they found my father, and beckoned him back home.

＊

My father did return to us the next day, with Old Mrs. Tulloch by his side. He lifted his damaged sea chest and placed it back in the bottom of the closet. Then he whispered something in my mother's ear, and she nodded her head.

"Isla," he said, "your mother and I are going out. Mrs. Tulloch will look after you and Callan."

The old lady made herself at home, pulling out her bag of yarn and two pairs of long, thin needles. "I'll teach you how to knit," she said with a smile, "and we'll bake bere bannocks with butter and jam to eat with our lunch."

"I don't want bere bannocks for lunch," I said, though, in truth, they were a favorite of mine. I ignored Mrs. Tulloch, speaking directly to my father. "I don't want to stay with her." I was worried that my parents would start fighting again as soon as they were out of our earshot. "I want to go with you and Mama."

"Isla—"

My name tapered off his tongue like a sigh. He rubbed his palm against the stubble of his beard. He looked tired, though whether it was because he had stayed out all night or because I was questioning his authority, I couldn't tell. "You need to stay with Mrs. Tulloch and help her look after Callan."

He turned toward the door, calling over his shoulder as he and my mother walked away. "We'll be home soon."

I don't know where my parents went or what they did, but after that day, things seemed to relax between them, and our house seemed happy once more. My mother cooked my father's favorite meals, and he spoke softly to her, lingering longer than usual when he kissed her before he left for work. My mother, brother, and I stayed close to the protected waters of Linklet Bay, and my father rewarded our obedience by taking our entire family to the western shore to celebrate Callan's first birthday. He wouldn't let us swim in the ocean, claiming the late autumn waters had grown too cold, but he allowed my mother to spend a few hours wandering the coast alone while he entertained us on the field adjacent to the rocky beach, laughing as Callan chased after the wild sheep. My mother had packed a picnic basket filled with cold slices of mutton, late-season berries, and fudge cakes for dessert. She placed a blue and white candle on top of Callan's cake and lit the wick. The flame glowed, bright and orange, a tiny mirror of the sun setting behind us in the west, and I watched as both lights were extinguished by the breezes that blew across the sea.

When I look back on those few peaceful weeks of our life, they shimmer like drops of sunlight sparkling on the water, dotting my memory with the color and warmth of the pink and yellow wildflowers that grow along the bluffs. I didn't know then that those carefree days were simply the calm before the storm, warning us, as the red morning sun warns sailors, of a treacherous tempest to come.

Four

Winter blew in, wet and wild, and with it came the long-tailed ducks and great northern divers that mark the change of the seasons. The simmer dim had been replaced by dark, mournful skies, and the clouds shed snowflake tears, each one melting over the black rocks like drops of spilled ink.

"Are you excited for our trip to Mainland?" my father asked one evening as he sat by the fire smoking his pipe and watching me play on the floor with Callan.

I nodded my head. We had skipped our holiday visit the year before because Callan had just been born, and I couldn't wait to return. Kirkwall, the Mainland town where my grandparents and uncles lived, was beautiful at Yuletide, the shops and houses along its narrow streets bright with candles and evergreen boughs.

My father picked up my little brother and swung him through the air. "And do you think Callan is ready for his first Ba'?" he asked as the baby giggled with delight.

 Kelly Jarvis

I laughed along with them. The Kirkwall Ba' was a Christmas and New Year's tradition dating back to the 19th century. Each year, hundreds of men would gather in front of St. Magnus Cathedral in the center of town to take part in a brutal show of their physical prowess and intellectual trickery. The Uppies, born south of the Mercat Cross, and the Doonies, born to the north, would compete to carry the season's hand-stitched leather ball to their goals on opposite ends of town. There were no rules and no referees, and the men's clothing would be ripped and tattered by the press of the scrum, which often lasted for hours. My father had always lifted me up to watch as the ball was tossed into the air to begin the game, and I would cling to him while the cathedral bells rang, and the spectators cheered, and the players pushed each other back and forth, surging up and down the crowded streets with the force of ocean currents.

I had never seen my father take part in the Kirkwall Ba', but tales of his performance fueled our family legends. According to his stories, one year, long before I was born, he had wrestled against the other players for more than seven hours before finally smuggling the ball out from the scrum by hiding it beneath his jersey. When he had broken free from the pack, he had run in the opposite direction of Kirkwall Bay, all the way to the wall at Mackinson's Corner, touching the ball against the goal to win the game. His brothers had hoisted him on their shoulders and carried him back to Broad Street where he had been declared the year's winner and made to host the spirited afterparty which had famously lasted for three days' time.

My father placed Callan back down on the rug and puffed on his pipe. "This year when we visit Mainland," he said, "we're going to look for a new home. Don't you think it would be fun to grow up in Kirkwall?"

"No."

It was my mother who answered, though my father had clearly been speaking to me. She was standing at the sink washing dishes while my father supervised Callan and me in front of the fire, but our cottage was small, and, apart from our bedrooms, there were few places for private conversations.

"They have schools in Kirkwall, Isla," my father continued, pretending he had not heard my mother's sharp and unsolicited reply. "Wouldn't you like to go to school with other children?"

I had always wanted to go to school. We had a Primary School on North Ronaldsay, but only two children attended, so my mother had decided to keep me home and teach me herself. We spent long hours combing the coastal beaches, learning about the turning tides and the wildlife that lived in the water. My mother had even taken me to the standing stone, a slab of stone that rises thirteen feet into the skies above North Ronaldsay. We had stood in its lee, looking across the open field that sloped down to the sea, identifying the far-off shapes of the other islands in our archipelago. My mother had taught me to use the stone to chart the yearly path of the sun, and on the shortest day of the year, we had stood before it, watching in awe as the midwinter light shone directly through the small hole in the standing stone's surface.

 Kelly Jarvis

My mother knew more about the seas and skies than any teacher could have, but she had little interest in reading and writing, and she had left me to the discover the secrets of language on my own. I wondered what it would be like to have a real teacher who would read me stories and help me practice my penmanship so I that could write my own stories in a legible hand.

A loud sound filled the kitchen as my mother set a plate down on the counter with more force than was necessary. She turned to face my father.

"*This* is our home," she said.

He didn't look at her as he responded. "We agreed we would move to Mainland when the children were ready for school."

"*I* am their school," my mother said, lifting her chin with stubborn pride.

My father had little to complain about regarding our education. My mother had taught me well, and everyone on our island commented on how smart I was. One of our neighbors, an older boy twelve years of age, had spent two years in residence at Kirkwall Grammar School, but I could already read and comprehend information much better than he could, and my father knew it.

He slowly turned to meet my mother's gaze. Callan, who had been crawling around the floor chasing after a ball, suddenly stilled, as though even at his tender age, he could sense the unspoken tension building between my parents.

"Isla needs to go to school with children her own age," my father said, "and Callan needs to be around people."

"He's only a pup—"

"He's a *child*," my father interrupted, standing up when my mother rolled her grey eyes at his correction. "Callan is over a year old now, and he hasn't yet said his first word."

It wasn't exactly true. Callan refused to speak the words my father tried to coax out of him, words like "Mama," "Papa," "Isla," "boat," and "ball," but he was proficient in a language all his own, communicating with a string of meaningful clicks and grunts. Each time Callan saw a seal breach the water's surface he would purse his lips together and make a puckering sound of recognition, and when he was hungry, his request for food was a deep growl that curled from the back of his throat.

"*This* is our home," my mother repeated.

She clicked her tongue against the roof of her mouth twice, her call for Callan. He slid over to her, and she picked him up, carrying him into his room and closing the door. My father said no more, but I knew from the way he glared into the flames of the fire that the discussion of where our family was going to live was far from over.

*

For days, I remained on my best behavior, waiting for an argument that never came. I hated it when my parents shouted at each other, but the newfound silence between them seemed far worse than the familiar sounds of their fighting. My father continued to talk about moving to Mainland like it was a forgone conclusion, my mother

 Kelly Jarvis

continued to say we would never leave North Ronaldsay, and I continued to smile and nod, wondering what was going to happen to our family if my parents failed to reach an agreement. Sometimes, I hoped my mother would prevail because I loved our little island, and I could not imagine her being happy in the crowded streets of Kirkwall. Sometimes, I hoped my father would claim victory because I knew how much he missed his family, and I dreamed of going to school with my cousins and friends.

"Kirkwall isn't such a bad place to live," I told my mother one day, as we were cleaning up after lunch. We had spent the morning swimming in rough waters, something that always made her happy, and I thought her good mood would provide the perfect opportunity to soften the deepening standoff between her and my father. "It might be fun to go to school and learn new things."

My mother lifted her stormy eyes to look at me. She said nothing, but I felt the heat of her anger burn against my cheeks. She stacked our clean plates and glasses in the cabinet and told me to look after Callan until my father came home from work.

"North Ronaldsay is nice too," I said. The last thing I wanted was for her to think I was taking my father's side. "Mama—"

She clicked her tongue and smacked her lips together, a sound that silenced me in an instant. Then she walked out the door, heading toward the red glow of the sun which was already setting in the dark winter skies.

That night, I dreamed I was caught in a whirlpool, its currents pulling me under, its water squeezing the air from my lungs. When I woke up, I was twisted in a tangled knot of blankets. My mother was by my side. She smoothed my sheets and stroked my hair. She smelled of the night and the sea and the wet rocks that line the shore.

I listened to the comforting ebb and flow of her breath as I fell back into a dreamless sleep.

Five

My mother began to spend more time on the wild, western shores, leaving Callan in my care for an hour or so before my father came home each night. I often wouldn't see her again until the next morning after my father had left for work, though I sometimes dreamed that she curled beside me while I was in bed, the gravelly notes of her lullabies drifting over me like enchanted bubbles of protection.

One rainy evening, my father returned from the fields with Dr. Sutherland, who kept an office in town, but often travelled door to door with his little black bag full of medicines. I had always liked Dr. Sutherland, even though my mother didn't trust him. He had a long, white beard and a deep, jolly laugh, and he always did his best to make me feel better when I had fallen ill.

"Whit like the day, Isla?" Dr. Sutherland asked, "how are you?" He slipped a butterscotch candy from his pocket and handed it to me with a smile. "Your father tells me you've been helping him look after Callan."

I beamed with pride. I knew my father counted on me to take care of things in my mother's absence, but it gave me great pleasure to learn that he had been bragging of my household contributions to his friends.

Dr. Sutherland whistled a sea shanty as he removed some instruments from his bag, wiping them down with alcohol and lining them up across a metal tray he had placed on our kitchen table. I watched him with interest, wondering why he had stopped by and what he planned to do with his sharp and shiny tools.

"Where's your mother tonight?" he asked me.

"She went for a walk by the ocean," I said. It was the truth, and though the words revealed little about what had been happening in my house over the last few weeks, Dr. Sutherland nodded at me with a sad smile, his eyes full of understanding.

He lifted Callan from the floor, bouncing him on his knee until my brother's laughter filled the cottage. Callan's soft white fur had long since molted, and a mop of black hair, the same color as our father's, crowned his head. Callan would grow into a handsome man with our father's strong jawline and broad shoulders, but his eyes would always carry the stormy grey clouds that came from our mother.

I felt my father's hand on my shoulder and turned to find him holding a book of Orkney folklore. It had a faerie on the cover, a short, ugly being with red eyes, green teeth, and brown, woolen mittens. My father had told me stories about the faeries and trows of Orkney, but I had never read about them in a book. New books were hard to come by on North Ronaldsay, and my hands trembled beneath the weight of the unexpected gift.

 Kelly Jarvis

"Be a good girl," my father said, kissing the top of my head, "and go read this in your bedroom."

I thanked him and skipped down the hallway, excited to bury myself in tales of changelings and faery circles, but when I placed my hand on the knob of my bedroom door, something made me hesitate. The skin on the back of my neck bristled, and I couldn't stop myself from looking back over my shoulder toward the kitchen where my father stood next to Dr. Sutherland and Callan.

I saw a silver flash in the corner of my eye, like a minnow darting through the shallows. Dr. Sutherland had flicked his scalpel and clipped the webbing between Callan's thumb and forefinger.

There was a moment of stunned silence.

Then Callan's scream of pain ripped through the air.

I dropped my new book to the floor, wanting to run down the hall and rescue my brother from the doctor's savage assault, but suddenly my mother was in the doorway, as though Callan's cry had conjured her from the wet mists that purled along the shoreline. I froze in place, waiting to see what she would do.

She flew toward Callan with a desperate howl, and I watched as my father shoved her backward, rising between her and her child like an immovable barrier of stone.

I backed into the corner and began to cry.

My mother bared her teeth. She snarled in disgust. She scratched and kicked at my father, knocking over the lamps and chairs.

"Stop, please!" my father pleaded, his words an order and a prayer. "Please! Just stop and listen to me!"

But my mother would not stop. She broke free of his grasp, lunging around him to reach Callan, and my father threw her across the room, pushing her against the wall with the full force of his strength. He clasped his powerful hands around her wrists and pinned her in place, trying to explain, in a calm and soothing manner at odds with the ferocity of his grip, that Dr. Sutherland was not hurting Callan.

My mother arched her back and flailed helplessly against him. She screeched and sobbed like a wounded animal, but the steadfast doctor continued to slice Callan's gossamer skin with his silver tools, and my father refused to let my mother go.

It felt like an eternity before the webbing between each of Callan's fingers and toes had been clipped away, the bleeding wounds sewed closed with the doctor's needle and thread. When the grueling procedure was complete, it was Dr. Sutherland who comforted Callan, wrapping his hands and feet in layers of white gauze and rubbing his back until his sobs settled into deep, contented sighs. My mother's knees had buckled beneath her, and my father pressed her against the floor, still holding her wrists so that she couldn't move.

Dr. Sutherland carried Callan to his crib, and then knelt down next to me, offering me his hand. It was large and calloused, like my father's, with wide spaces between each of his fingers.

"Callan is fast asleep, Isla," he said, his words sweet, like butterscotch. "And now it's time for you to get ready for bed. Everything will be fine when you wake up in the morning."

I didn't believe him, but I let Dr. Sutherland take me into my room and tuck me beneath my covers. He read me a faery story from the new book my father had given me. Then he sat with me, whistling his sea chanty, until I pretended to fall asleep.

All night I listened as my mother's tears rolled on and on, like the relentless waves that endlessly pound against our islands' sandy shores.

Six

There was an eerie silence in the house when I woke up the next morning. I found my father sitting at the kitchen table, his hands wrapped around a cup of strong, black coffee. Callan was sitting in his high chair, a bowl of porridge perched on his tray. His little fork and spoon, which were stamped with silver starfish, rested next to the bowl. Callan couldn't grasp the utensils because his hands were still bandaged from the procedure he had endured the night before, so he bent his neck toward the tray, lapping up his breakfast with his pink tongue.

My father poured me a glass of milk and placed a few cold sausage links on my plate. I was hungry, but when I cut into the meat, I felt sick, so I pushed my food away and watched the steam rise from my father's cup as he rummaged in our bedrooms, packing some of our clothes into a small bag. He didn't speak as he washed Callan's face and buttoned us into our coats. He slung the bag over his shoulder, lifted Callan in his arms, and took my hand, leading me out the door.

   Kelly Jarvis

It was nearing midday and the sun had risen, throwing his weak winter light over the frosted vegetation. Our feet left a trail of prints on the untouched rime of the lane. We passed through the center of town and turned toward the docks where the Mainland Ferry was preparing to pull out of port, but when my father stepped onto the plank leading up to the ferry, I stopped walking and pulled against his hand.

"Come, Isla," he said, tugging on my arm and using the tone of voice that usually prompted my immediate compliance.

I refused to move.

He shifted the bag on his shoulder and leaned down to pick me up and carry me onto the boat, but I stopped his movement with a question.

"Why did you let Dr. Sutherland hurt Callan?"

I was afraid to ask him why he had hurt our mother. In my child's mind, the two things twisted together into a terrible nightmare I did not yet understand.

"Isla—"

I wrenched myself away from him. A tear rolled down my cheek, and when my father saw I was crying, his irritation with my defiance disappeared. He knelt on the wooden dock, balancing Callan on one knee. A cold breeze blew off the water. It twirled through our hair and made my brother laugh. My father reached out to me, holding his palm upward in invitation.

"Callan will be fine, Isla," he said, softly stroking my arm when I did not take his hand. "Your brother isn't going to remember what happened. Dr. Sutherland performed an operation that will help him grow, and now you and I need to bring him to Kirkwall so he can heal."

"What about Mama?" I asked, my voice breaking. I stared at my father's hands as I spoke. They caressed me lovingly, but I couldn't stop myself from remembering how forcefully those hands had held my mother down. Although I had grown up listening to the sounds of my parents arguing, I had never seen my father raise his hands against my mother before, and I wished I could erase the terrible memory of it from my mind.

My father didn't respond, and after a few minutes, I glanced up at him. He had dark circles under his eyes, and the stubble of his beard was peppered with grey. He looked at me like he wanted to say something profound, but he swallowed, and when he spoke, I knew he was only telling me what I needed to hear.

"Your mother will be fine."

The ferry's whistle filled the air, and my father stood up, the decisive tone of his voice returning. "We're going to Kirkwall," he said. "Once we're settled there, I'll come back to North Ronaldsay and bring your mother home to us."

"What if she won't leave?" I asked. My mother had never ventured from our small island before.

"She will," he promised. "But right now, the ferry is departing, and we have to be on it." The skipper had already loosened the ropes that held the boat against its pilings. "Come, Isla." This time, his words were a plea rather than a command.

I thought about running away from him. I knew that my mother was likely walking along the wild western shores, and

Kelly Jarvis

I wanted to find her and let her hold me as we floated over the waves, but I also knew that my father needed me to be strong and constant, a safe place to anchor amid the swirling storm.

I followed him up the plank.

We found our seats as the boat pulled out of the harbor. Callan waved his bandaged hands at the black headed gulls that flew in the ferry's wake, and I watched the only home I had ever known fade into the distance as we headed south beneath heavy morning skies.

✳

My uncles were waiting for us when we disembarked in Kirkwall. One of them lifted me onto his shoulders and carried me through town, trotting over the cobblestone sidewalks and singing a holiday tune. The clang of hammers pounded through the thin December air as the owners of shops and houses along the route of the upcoming Ba' built barricades to prevent the players from falling through glass windows and doors.

We walked past St Magnus Cathedral, its spire reaching up to scrape the evening sky. It had been built by Vikings in the 12th century, and its red and yellow sandstone slabs made me think of the medieval castles in my fairy tale books. One of my cousins had once told me that the cathedral had its own dungeon, and that a box filled with skulls and bones had been found hidden inside one of its columns. I liked to look at the faces of the men, women, and animals that had been carved into the stonework on the outside of the steeple. I loved the bright colors of the stained glass windows and the chiming of the tower's bells, but I had trouble sitting still on the cold, hard benches, and I was always eager to dart outside and fill my lungs with fresh air whenever I attended services with my father's family.

My grandparents' house was located just south of the cathedral, on a blind street set back from the paths the teams would take during the Kirkwall Ba'. Since there was no need to barricade the house against the onslaught of the scrum, my grandmother had set flickering candles in each of the windows, and their flames danced, bright in the midwinter night, as we approached the door.

"Weel beuy, whit's deuan the day?" my grandfather said as he pulled my father into a warm embrace. Apart from his white hair and the lines that crossed his leathery skin, he looked just like his sons, and he was overjoyed to see my father, the only one of his children who didn't reside in Kirkwall. My grandmother, an elegant woman with bleached blonde hair twisted in a pile on top of her head, cried when she saw Callan. She kissed the bandages on his hands and feet, and her dark, red lipstick stained the gauze, so that I could not tell where the marks of his dried blood ended and the marks of her makeup began.

My uncle had carried me into the house, ducking so we would fit through the door, and my grandmother admonished him to put me down, frowning at my disheveled appearance. It was the night before Christmas Eve, and my father's extended family would all be gathering at my grandparents' house for

Kelly Jarvis

dinner, so she took me into one of the bedrooms and did her best to make me look presentable, brushing and plaiting my long, brown hair which had been tangled by the ocean winds.

"Sit still," she said when I complained that the braids made my scalp ache. She continued to tug and twist until she had tamed my errant curls with her comb and elastic bands.

My family's holiday celebrations were filled with music and laughter, and on Christmas morning, we found a pile of presents beneath my grandparents' tree. My cousins delighted in their new clothes and toys, but although I had received a beautiful, leather-bound collection of Hans Christian Anderson's fairy tales, I couldn't even bring myself to look at the pictures. The only present I had wanted had been left alone on the shores of North Ronaldsay, and there were no grey seals in the crowded streets of Kirkwall who might bring her to me to make my Christmas wish come true.

Seven

The week between Christmas and New Year's Day was a torrent of activity in my grandparents' house, with a rotating cast of cousins to play with and grown-ups to listen to. My father was already working odd jobs at the dock with the hopes of finding permanent employment so we could stay in Kirkwall, which meant Callan and I were left to navigate the long, dark days on our own.

The Doonies had reigned victorious in the Christmas Ba', the men's and boys' teams both plunging the season's leather-covered cork balls into the harbor to roll and bounce on the waves. The Uppies were thirsty to win the rematch scheduled for New Year's Day, and my uncle's sons, John and Ian, who were taking part in the Boys Ba' for the first time, talked endlessly about altering their failed Christmas Day strategies so they could effectively defeat their opponents and reach their inland goal at Mackinson's Corner.

I usually enjoyed the excitement of the Ba', but this year, when my father had offered to take me to Mercat Cross on

Kelly Jarvis

Christmas Day to watch the contest unfold, I had elected to stay behind. I had covered my ears all afternoon, hoping to block out the shouting of the crowds, trying to escape the loud cheers which echoed all the way down the narrow street to my grandparents' house. When the scrum had finally ended, I felt nothing but relief. I didn't care that the Doonies had won or that the Uppies had sworn revenge. The last thing I wanted to talk about was the upcoming rematch, and I wished my cousins would find a different topic of conversation.

My grandmother did her best to distract me from the boys' strategic planning, keeping me busy so I wouldn't have time to think about how much I missed my mother. She asked me to help her in the kitchen, but I was clumsy and spilled an entire bowl of her carefully measured batter all over the counter. She took me to a carol service at St. Magnus Cathedral, but the hollow clanging of the bells only made me feel lonely. She showed me the twinkling lights that had been strung across the rooftops of Kirkwall, but I looked beyond them toward the subtle streaks of purple, pink, and green that billowed in the northern sky.

One afternoon, I was playing quietly in the corner of the bedroom where Callan and I had been sleeping all week, when John and Ian tumbled through the doorway. They had been wrestling each other for control of the leather ball that was their favorite plaything at my grandmother's house. John pushed Ian, who was two years his junior, into the corner of the wardrobe, knocking the limpet shell I had placed on top of it to the floor. It was a beautiful shell, with iridescent grey swirls on the outside of its cone and a soft blue pattern underneath. I had placed it in my pocket the morning we left North Ronaldsay, and I had held it in my hands every night since, tracing its swirls with my finger when I was unable to sleep. Ian stumbled backward as he tried to maintain his grip on the ball, and I heard my shell crush to pieces beneath his feet.

A hot and pulsating rage rose up in my throat like bile. I flew at Ian, sinking my teeth into the flesh of his arm.

"Let go of me," he yelped in surprise. He grabbed my braids with his free hand and yanked my neck back. John had just managed to pull us apart as our grandmother rushed into the room.

"What's going on in here?" she asked, tapping the wooden spoon she had been using in the kitchen against the side of the wardrobe to command our attention. She wore a decorative apron over her silk blouse, and its ruffles were dotted with flour and sugar.

John, Ian, and I all looked at each other, not knowing what to say. Our grandmother tapped her spoon on the wardrobe again, harder this time.

We all flinched at the sound.

"I want to know what's going on, right now," she demanded. Her eyes roamed from the leather ball that had been discarded on the floor to the tuft of my hair still clenched in Ian's fist to the broken remnants of my limpet shell sticking up from the tufts of the carpet.

"She bit me," Ian finally explained, trying to justify why he had been fighting with his younger cousin. He held up his arm to show our grandmother the marks my teeth had left

 Kelly Jarvis

behind. My bite had broken his skin, and a trickle of his blood dripped onto the rug.

My grandmother's face turned deathly pale, and she grabbed me, bringing her spoon down across my knuckles. "Wild thing!" she yelled, as she smacked me a second, third, and fourth time, bruising my hand and sending waves of pain up and down my arm. "Young ladies do not behave like animals!"

She sent the boys outside to continue their game and told me I was to stay alone in the bedroom until my father came home from work. I had never been in trouble at my grandmother's house before, and I was worried my father was going to be angry with me. A red welt bloomed across the back of my hand, but when I tried to shake away its sting, my movements only made the aching worse. I rubbed the tears from my face and sank to the floor to pick up my broken shell, thinking that as long as I could glue it back together, my grandmother's unfair treatment of me wouldn't matter.

When I touched the fragile pieces, they crumbled to dust beneath my fingers.

❋

"Why did you bite your cousin?" my father asked me later that evening. My grandmother had dragged Ian and me into the living room to recount my crime to both of our fathers. She held Ian's arm out as evidence against me.

The clock on the mantle ticked in time with the throbbing of my injured hand. I could feel the eyes of all the grownups in the room looking at me. My father and uncle both stood with their arms crossed in front of their chests. They wore serious expressions on their faces, and they seemed impossibly tall. My uncle called Ian over to him, examining the wound I had inflicted.

"Why did you bite your cousin, Isla?" my father repeated when he saw the scars of my teeth on Ian's skin.

"Did you do something to upset her?" my uncle asked Ian.

"That hardly matters," my grandmother interjected, steadfast in her condemnation of my behavior. "A child her age should not biting *anyone* for *any* reason."

"We were just playing," Ian said. Although he had been angry with me when I first bit him, he felt bad for telling on me, and he didn't want me to get into any more trouble. "It doesn't even hurt."

"It's a *barbaric* thing to do," my grandmother whispered to my father, her voice full of judgement. "If you don't put a stop to this, she'll turn out *exactly* like her mother."

Every muscle in my father's body went rigid as he turned to look at my grandmother. "Don't—"

"You have to punish her to teach her the difference between right and wrong."

"I'm sure she didn't mean—"

"She can't go around *biting* people!"

My father exhaled loudly in response to my grandmother's continued interruptions. He closed his eyes, and a shadow of regret passed over his face. When he opened them, his expression was stoic.

"Come with me, Isla," he said, taking me outside into the darkening night.

Eight

We walked in silence until we reached the crowded streets of downtown Kirkwall where winter winds whistled through the corridors created by the makeshift barriers. The low skies were streaked with heavy, wet clouds that pressed against our shoulders. I saw a procession of men in the distance, performing their annual ritual designed to rid the town of malicious spirits and welcome in the New Year. They carried tall torches, sweeping the skies with their fire, and one of them swung a flaming ball attached to a long chain. I knew the men would hurl the fireball into the water as a way of protecting the fishermen's livelihoods, and I wanted to watch the flames sizzle and smoke when they touched the bay, but my father turned me into a little shop that sold coffee and tea. He ordered me a steaming mug of hot chocolate and found us a seat by a large window overlooking the bustle and hurry of Kirkwall. He took his flask from his pocket and poured its contents into an empty glass. His whisky shimmered like liquid gold in the dim light.

Kelly Jarvis

My father took a long drink and set his glass back down on the table.

"Why did you bite your cousin, Isla?" he asked me for the third time that night. His long, hard days away from home, away from my mother, were written in deep lines across his face.

I let my eyes fall to the paper placemat beneath my cup. The whipped cream on top of my hot chocolate had already begun to melt, and a glob of it slipped down the side of the mug, staining the corner of the paper. My father tapped his fingers on the table as he waited for me to answer him, his rhythm steady and impatient.

"I don't know," I finally whispered.

I couldn't find the words to explain what had happened. I hadn't meant to bite Ian, and I knew I shouldn't have done it, but when his foot had shattered my limpet shell, something had loosened inside me. I had acted on instinct, without stopping to think about the consequences.

My father stared at me until I looked up at him. "You can't bite people," he said firmly. "When we go back to the house, you will apologize to Ian, and you will to apologize to your grandmother." He leaned forward so he could convey the serious nature of his edict without raising his voice in the crowded shop. "We're guests in their home, Isla, and I need to know that you'll behave yourself when I'm away at work."

I nodded my head, a lump of emotion rising in my throat. I would have agreed to any punishment he might have meted out, if only it would erase his expression of disappointment. He took another long sip of his whiskey and refilled his glass.

I moved my finger through a fresh drop of whipped cream that had fallen onto the table.

"Papa," I began, my heart fluttering in my chest. My voice was small and frail against the echo and din of the tea shop.

"What's wrong, Isla?" he asked.

My grandmother's angry words were still throbbing in my ears. They had caused me more pain than her physical reprimand, and they had made me feel ashamed. I tried to force my question from my dry and heavy tongue, though I wasn't sure I wanted to hear my father's answer.

"Do you—" I paused and took a deep breath. "Do you think I'm a wild thing?"

He didn't reply, but he placed his hand over mine, his calloused fingers brushing against the red welt left by my grandmother's spoon. He turned to look out the window where a bright, full moon was rising.

"Do you know what a selkie is, Isla?"

I was confused by his question. Of course I knew what a selkie was. All Orkney children did. We were raised on stories of the seal folk who swam off the coasts of our islands. We knew that every seventh summer at the simmer dim, the selkies would shed their seal skins and walk like humans upon the land, dancing and laughing in the twilight dusk.

My father cleared his throat. "Do you remember when I told you that I first saw your mother dancing on the western shores of North Ronaldsay?"

I didn't understand why my father was asking me questions instead of answering mine, but his voice had taken

Kelly Jarvis

on the cadence he used to tell me stories, and I nodded, settling against its deep and familiar tone.

"It was seven summer solstices before I would see your mother again," he said, "but I recognized her instantly. I would have known her grey eyes anywhere. I was no longer a boy, and I wasn't afraid of her anymore, so I walked up to her and introduced myself. Her skin smelled like the pale ocean flowers that grow along the coastline."

He finished the whisky in his glass before continuing. "We spent the long simmer dim together, swimming in the churning froth of the tides. She showed me where to find the razor clams that burrow in coarse sands, and I wove her a ring of knotted seaweed, kissing her as I slipped it over her finger. When the moon found her hour of patchy darkness in the sky, we stretched out over the wet sand and let the surf lull us to sleep."

He shook his head as though the beautiful memory caused him great pain.

"When I woke up," he said, "she was gone."

"Where did she go?" I asked.

He turned away from the window to look at me. A few strands had loosened themselves from the intricate braids my grandmother had woven in my hair that morning, and he tucked them behind my ear.

"For seven more years, I waited," he said, ignoring my question. "While my brothers and my friends finished school, got married, and started their families, I waited for your mother to return."

"Return from where?" I asked again, growing frustrated with his dismissal of my inquiries.

He placed his empty glass on the table and brought his flask directly to his lips, tipping his head back to release the final drops.

"North," he answered, screwing the cap back on the flask and placing it into his jacket pocket.

One of my books at home was filled with maps, and I had seen pictures of Shetland in the oceans to our north, and beyond that, several small Scandinavian islands in the Norwegian Sea. I wondered if my mother and her family had come from one of those places. Surely that made more sense than the story my father was telling, the story that made it sound like my mother was a selkie.

"The next time I saw your mother," my father continued, "I knew I couldn't let her slip away from me again, so I married her, and the following year, you slid down from your moonbeam." He smiled at me. "*You* made us a family."

I knew that no matter how old Callan and I grew, my father would never stop telling his tall tales about how I had come from heaven and my brother had come from the sea, but I couldn't make sense of his reasons for pretending my mother had come from the pages of selkie folklore. I wondered if he was trying to tell me that my grandmother was right. Maybe I was a wild thing, just like my mother. Maybe I had inherited her temper, and no matter how hard I tried, I would never escape the type of savage confrontations I had listened to all my life because I, too, was half-feral and doomed to act like an animal.

My father watched my worries cross my face like storm clouds. He tried to smile again, but his eyes were full of something that looked like sorrow.

 Kelly Jarvis

"You want to know if I could ever love a wild thing," he said, articulating the unspoken meaning of the question I had been trying to ask him. He leaned close to me, his thumb stroking the pulsating scar on the back of my hand. I could smell the whiskey on his breath.

"Your mother is the most beautiful and wild creature I have ever known, Isla, and I love her more than life itself."

I was eight years old, and I no longer thought that faerie legends about selkie brides were true, but that night, I let his story comfort me because I needed to believe that my father could love a wild thing like me.

I lingered over my hot chocolate to delay my promised apologies to Ian and my grandmother as long as I could, and when I had finished, my father said we could walk along the path that ran parallel to Kirkwall Bay before heading south past St. Magnus Cathedral and back to my grandparents' house. The torchlight procession I had wanted to see had long since ended, but the dark clouds that had haunted the evening parted like a curtain, and the stars glowed silver against clear skies of slate and midnight blue. The full moon floated high over Kirkwall's low skyline, and as we turned the corner and looked down the hill toward the harbor, we saw her reflection shimmering in the still waters of the bay. Two moons, mirror images of each other, glinted like precious jewels in the crowns of deep, dark night. My father put his arm around me.

"It's called a Selkie Moon," he said pointing to the pool of light in the harbor. I had seen the moon throw her sparkling path over the choppy waters that surrounded our North Ronaldsay home, but I had never seen her shine, round and full beneath the surface, as she did that night in the protected bay.

"The selkies come from miles away to bathe their seal skins in the full moon's magic," my father explained. He struck a match on the rough, wool sleeve of his coat and lit the pipe he had taken from his pocket. Soon the earthy scent of tobacco and the sweet odor of cherries warmed the damp winter air. "If a fisherman wants to catch a selkie without waiting seven years until she dances on the beach during the summer solstice, all he has to do is find a Selkie Moon and steal one of the seal coats that has been hung on the seafoam to dry." He paused his speech to take a deep puff on his pipe, and the gleam from the embers illuminated the sharp lines of his jaw. "Once a fisherman has a selkie's skin in his possession, she can never leave him. The two of them will be bound together for the rest of their lives."

I watched dark shadows slip through the water, imagining each one might be a grey seal who had come to launder her silky coat in a magic beam of moonlight. I wondered if it was possible that my own mother might have been a seal, long ago, in another lifetime, before I was born. I wondered if it was possible that my own father might have stolen her skin and hidden it away so she could never return to her home. It seemed cruel to take a selkie's skin without her consent, to condemn a wild ocean creature to a lonely life on dry land.

"The selkies sing to their watery moon just like our poets sing to the moon that hangs in our skies," my father continued, unbothered by the moral implications of his tale. His breath curled into the cold, night air like chimney smoke.

"We are all surrounded by darkness," he said. "And we are all drawn to the light."

All the selkie legends I had ever heard had been woven of threads both light and dark. They were love stories about beings from different worlds who came together to start their own families, but, in the end, when a selkie woman found the seal coat her husband had stolen from her, she almost always returned to the sea, leaving him and her half-human children behind. Panic rose in my heart as I realized my father might be telling me selkie stories as a way of letting me know that my mother had left us, and we would never see her again.

"I miss Mama," I whispered. In that moment, I would have gladly stolen her skin myself if only it would have forced her to come back to us.

"You have nothing to worry about, Isla." My father took my hand and steered us away from the harbor. I had to hurry to keep up with his long strides as we headed back toward St. Magnus Cathedral. "I've locked your mother's seal coat up tight and hidden the key where she'll never find it," he said. "She'll come back to us. She has no choice."

He winked at me as though we shared a great secret, and although I only half-believed my father's tale was true, his story seemed like a clue that might one day help me to glue my broken family back together again.

Nine

Callan and I stayed with my grandparents for more than three months, and I tried my best to be good. My grandmother was kind to me, but she was constantly correcting my behavior, even as she let my brother and the other boys run wild.

"Young ladies do not climb over fences," she would warn me as we walked through town to complete her household errands.

"Young ladies do not ask for second helpings," she would say, pushing away the platter of smoked crab claws when I tried to fill my bowl with more.

"Young ladies speak when spoken to," she would tell me each time I answered her questions with a sullen stare.

Callan's stitches eventually dissolved, leaving fresh white flecks of skin in their place. No one who met him on Mainland would ever know what he had been through, but I would always be able to read the scars of his transformation written in the absence between his fingers and toes.

 Kelly Jarvis

The red welt on the back of my hand turned purple and then faded into brown-flecked shades of green and blue. I imagined that the marks my father must have left upon my mother when he had restrained her that horrible night had faded in the same way, and it made me feel strangely close to her, as though the dwindling bruises on our bodies proved we would always be connected because we shared the same skin.

My father alternated his time between working and taking long trips back to North Ronaldsay. I imagined him pulling golden apologies out of the air and laying them like bandages over my mother's raw memory of what he had done to her and Callan. On Sundays, when my grandmother brought me to St Magnus Cathedral, I prayed his words would work their magic, but deep down, I worried that both his betrayal, and my own, were unforgiveable. My father had brought Dr. Sutherland into our house against my mother's wishes. My father had thrown my mother across the room, wrestling her into submission as the doctor cut away her child's flesh. My father had used me as a pawn to lure my mother from North Ronaldsay, and I had willingly followed him to Kirkwall instead of staying on our island to comfort the woman who had carried me in her womb and birthed me into life, the woman who had always been my safe space and my home.

"She'll come back to us, Isla," my father would say each time I woke up in the middle of the night wailing for my mother. "Don't cry. I promise you I'll fix this. She'll come back to us, and everything will be alright."

$\mathcal{I}$t was mid-March before winter's dark hold upon the skies began to fade, and the strengthening sun brought forth an explosion of wildflowers, each one a burst of pink and purple in the cracks and crevices of Kirkwall's grey cobblestones. I loved the stray weeds that pushed their way into my grandmother's formal garden, which was organized into tidy sections and long, straight rows. It was one of my chores to help my grandmother water her plants and make sure nothing disturbed her cultivated blooms, but whenever she turned her back, I used my little spade to dig wells around the weeds, filling each space with nourishing water to help the unwanted blossoms grow.

One afternoon, my father came home early from work and took Callan and me to a village on the isolated, western coast of Mainland. The air smelled of sea salt and spring rains, and the wide, open skies were streaked with shades of steel gray and buttery blue. We walked up a long, grassy hill where yellow coltsfoot, marsh marigolds, and Scottish primroses swayed in the winds.

At the top of the hill, on a bluff overlooking the storm-tossed North Atlantic, was a small house with a white-painted swing hung on the wide front porch. The sun and moon would rise over the hill behind the house and set in the rough ocean waters beneath the cliffs, making the swing on the front porch the perfect place to watch each bright, summer day transform itself into the glittering dusk of a simmer dim night.

The chains of the swing rattled in the sea breezes. The door of the house creaked opened.

"Welcome home," my father said.

It was the most beautiful home that I had ever seen, but more beautiful than the porch swing, the flowers, the sea, or the sky, was my mother, standing in the doorway, her loose curls blowing wild.

I held my breath, blinking away tears, hoping she wasn't a figment of my imagination. Then I ran to her and fell into her arms. Her salt water scent washed over me. She kissed me and hugged me, clicking for Callan who clamored up the steps to her, scraping his knees on the stones in his hurry to disappear into our mother's embrace.

My father stood apart from us, watching our reunion. In all my life, I never saw him cry, but that day, the rough March winds that blustered up from the sea gave his eyes a watery sheen. When he finally joined us, his feet were slow and heavy on the steps. He placed his hands, gently, around the three of us, stroking my mother's hair.

Callan and I nuzzled between them as they kissed each other like long-lost oceans that had finally found their shore.

Ten

O nly the strongest and most stubborn can survive along the bluffs on Mainland's west coast. They are dampened by rain and battered by wind, and people who walk too close to the edge can easily lose their footing and tumble into the perilous seas below. In the coming years, Callan and I would grow so sure-footed that we thought nothing of sliding down the steep paths to swim and play in the rolling breakers, though we never invited our school friends to join us.

It took several months for our family to settle into a routine in our new home, but, before long, Callan hardly remembered the rocky beaches on the western coast of North Ronaldsay where he used to chase after seaweed-eating sheep and propel himself though the waves with his webbed hands and feet. My mother did everything she could to delay my schooling as long as possible, so it wasn't until the second term began at the end of October that my father finally managed to enroll me. My grandmother had gifted me new clothes for the occasion, a pleated skirt and white blouse with a matching

Kelly Jarvis

ribbon to tie in my hair. My mother buttoned me into my old, grey dress on my first day of school instead, saying its woolen knit would keep me warm on our long walk to my classroom.

I had a leather satchel to hold my lunch, a notebook filled with blue-lined paper, and a small bag of yellow pencils, their lead tips filed into sharp points. In future years I would always begin school at the end of August when the first term started, but I would never forget the warm, russet colors and the scent of decaying autumn foliage that marked the initiation of my formal education.

I squeezed my mother's hand as we approached my new teacher to introduce ourselves. Callan, now almost two years old, darted ahead of us and clamored up and over the benches lined against the brick wall of the school.

"You must be our new student, Isla," the teacher said with a bright and welcoming smile.

My mother grunted softly, letting her tongue slap the back of her teeth to remind me of my manners.

"Pleased to meet you," I said.

I was nervous about spending the whole day away from my mother and brother, but when I saw my new classroom, my fears melted away. The back corner of the room had been fitted with tall shelves that held more books than I had ever seen in one place. Three girls my age were gathered around a reading table, and my teacher directed me to join them.

They all wore pleated skirts and had matching ribbons tied in their plaited hair.

"What's that?" one of them asked, laughing and pointing to the bracelet that circled my wrist. My mother had woven one for each of us from strands of dried seaweed she had collected along the shore. Their beautiful black and green vines twisted over and around each other, and their knots were held in place with a sticky film of algae. My mother had told me that if I felt sad or lonely while I was away at school, all I had to do was raise the bracelet to my face and inhale the briny, fresh scent of the sea. I loved my new bracelet, and knowing my mother wore an identical one had made me feel brave, but now that all the girls were staring at it, I grew uncomfortable. I wished I could disappear behind the tall shelf of books.

"Did you make that yourself?" another girl asked, and my new classmates burst into fresh giggles.

My cheeks burned red as I looked to the floor, self-consciously twirling the long, loose curls that fell over my shoulders. One of the girls, the tallest of the three, shushed the others and patted my arm.

"They're only trying to tell you how pretty your bracelet is," she said. "It's so unique."

Her words sounded kind, but there was something beneath the kindness that I couldn't identify. I looked out the window and watched as my mother, who had wrangled Callan into her arms, began her long walk back to our home on the bluffs.

A part of me wondered if she had been right about school all along.

❊

Kelly Jarvis

Although the teachers and students in my class were friendly, I couldn't help feeling like an outsider. The girls in my year all lived near the center of our village, and they and their families had known each other all their lives. Several of their fathers knew and liked my father, as everyone I had ever met on Orkney always did, but after-school activities took place under the watchful eyes of the mothers, and my mother had no interest in making new friends. Whenever we were asked to join, she would quietly vocalize her dissent to me, and I would have to decline the invitation, explaining that we had chores waiting for us at home. I usually didn't mind missing out because school days felt so long to me, and I looked forward to going home and swimming in the sea with my mother and brother, but sometimes, I would notice the other girls in my class whispering and laughing about things they had done together, and it made me feel sad and alone.

"What's so funny?" I would ask, hoping one of them would share the story so I could join in their giggling.

"Oh, Isla, we couldn't possibly explain," was the common reply. "You just had to be there."

I would twirl my pencil, drawing starfish and moor flowers along the borders of my assignments, wishing that my mother could be more like theirs.

✳

Despite my social struggles, I loved going to school. Moving to Mainland opened up a world beyond my father's imaginative stories and my mother's deep knowledge of the sea, a world of science and history and wonder. My class took field trips to the Brough of Birsay, an uninhabited tidal island off the north-west coast. We visited the Neolithic village of Skara Brae, a pre-historic settlement uncovered by a devastating storm. We toured the old Norse church and explored the Pictish graveyard. We deciphered Viking runes. We learned that the northern lights are called the aurora borealis, and that their ribbons of blue, green, and violet are caused by the sun's pull on the earth's magnetic field. We studied the cumulonimbus clouds that produce thunder and lightning and calculated the moon's influence on the tides. We read about the creatures that sail through foreign skies, and soon I could identify not only the hen harriers, puffins, and arctic terns native to Orkney, but also the monarch butterflies of North America, whose seasonal migration from their breeding grounds and back spans across generations.

My teacher tried to encourage my love of learning by letting me borrow books from our classroom library, and one day, instead of joining my mother and Callan in the sea, I brought a book with me to the water's edge and opened it up to read in the sun. My mother made a sour face as I recited a passage aloud to Callan, trying to show him how the small black marks on the page created wonderous tales that could be revisited again and again. My mother took the book from my hands and playfully tossed it onto the sand, pulling me back out toward the waves.

"Mama!"

 Kelly Jarvis

I laughed as she splashed us with foam. Then I let myself be carried away by the welcoming hands of the ocean. I dove beneath the surface, and when I came up for air, my mother nodded her head toward a red stripe of light painted across the horizon. "A storm is coming," I said, knowing that she was testing my knowledge of the things she had taught me and trying to remind me that I could learn more from reading the landscape than I could learn from reading a book. She smiled, and we spent an hour frolicking in the shallows with Callan before fat rain drops began to fall from the sky. I grabbed my book and scurried up the bluffs, but by the time I reached our house, the pages had been damaged beyond repair. Sea water and precipitation had soaked through the cover, leaving large, salty stains behind.

I thought I would have to scrape together the remains of my birthday money to pay for a classroom replacement, but when I penitently showed the ruined book to my teacher the next day, she said I could stay after school to help her clean the pages with a special solution instead. It took us a long time to repair the damage. We needed to apply a clear paste to each page, letting it dry in the sun before repeating the process on the following sheets of paper. After a few hours, the brown rings of salt left by the sea water had disappeared.

"It's as good as new," my teacher said, returning it back to the classroom shelf.

The next day, I opened the book at silent reading time. I had never gotten the chance to finish the story, and I longed to know how it ended. My stomach turned as the mingled odors of musty water and sterile detergent rose from its freshly cleaned pages. The book did not look damaged, but it had been scarred by its interaction with both salt and soap. My teacher had been wrong. The book was no longer as good as new.

I closed the cover and never opened it again.

Kelly Jarvis

Eleven

The year I turned eleven, one of my school friends invited our entire class to her birthday party at the park in the village. The wooden bridge that ran over the park's freshwater stream was going to be decorated with banners and balloons, and there was going to be music, games, and dancing. Best of all, my friend's mother, an accomplished baker, was going to bake a blackberry cake decorated with pink sugar roses.

"There will be older *and* younger siblings at the party," I told my mother, "so even Callan will have someone to play with."

The grey clouds of her eyes rolled upward in irritation at my whining tone, and she continued to debone the fish my father had caught for dinner without saying anything.

"Please, Mama."

I brought my tongue to the roof of my mouth and let it fall, creating the rippling sound I had used to call her before

I was old enough to understand words. "*All* the girls in my class are going."

My mother's harsh expression softened. I wondered if she missed her own sisters and cousins who had danced with her on the beach the night she had met my father. She never spoke about her family, and the only relatives I knew came from my father's side. Sometimes it seemed like my mother was the one who had fallen from a moonbeam in the sky, landing on North Ronaldsay just so my father could find her.

That night my mother took me down to the rocky beach below the bluffs and helped me gather handfuls of groatie buckies beneath a starlit sky. The small, pastel cowrie shells were notoriously difficult for beachcombers to find, but my mother knew exactly where to look. We washed them in sea water, polishing them on my mother's skirts until they gleamed. Then we piled them into a small, glass jar and tied a long, silk ribbon around the crystal stopper.

Groatie buckies had always been considered good luck on our islands, and I knew the beautiful treasure jar we created would be the perfect birthday gift for my friend.

On the morning of the party, I awoke to a terrible stench and wandered outside to find its source. My father was drinking his coffee on the porch. When he saw me, he tapped his knee, and I climbed up to sit on his lap like I used to do when I was young.

"What's that smell?" I asked, holding my nose closed as I spoke.

"It's coming from the whale," he said. He pointed toward the horizon where I could barely see a mound of rotting flesh

Kelly Jarvis

floating on the surface of the water. A humpback whale had died, and the body which had housed its soul was drifting helplessly in the ocean currents. I watched it undulate in the rolling swells, and my eyes grew wet with tears.

"Don't look so glum," my father teased, tousling my hair. "The winds will shift soon, and the smell will blow out to sea."

Although the air was putrid, it wasn't the smell that had upset me. I wasn't sure why the thought of a whale's death had made me so emotional. I was used to cleaning the fish my father killed, and I was old enough to understand the slabs of meat he brought home from the butcher shop had come from once-living animals, but all the humpback whales I had ever seen from the decks of the ferries that transported us between the islands had been so massive that I thought they must have lived forever, free from the mortal struggles of smaller prey.

I had read about humpback whales in school. I knew the females were gentle creatures who nursed and protected their calves until they were old enough to survive on their own. My father had told me a story about a humpback who had rescued a seal from an orca attack, and my mother had taken me past the break line on North Ronaldsay, teaching me to dive beneath the surface of the water so we could listen to the humpbacks sing. It was the male humpbacks who made music, she had told me, and I had always wondered if their somber voices, which vibrated through the waves like nautical bagpipes, were meant to comfort other solitary migrants who traversed the wide oceans looking for a place to call home.

My father lifted me off his lap and stood up. He was wearing his fisherman's gear, and I knew that meant he would spend all day toiling at sea, something he seemed to do more often since we had moved to the west coast of Mainland. "Stay out of the ocean today, Isla," he said, "and make sure your brother does the same. Sharks will be circling the carcass, and the waters will be dangerous." He kissed my cheek and headed down the stairs.

"Yes, Papa," I said, when he looked back over his shoulder to confirm I had heard and understood his command. On any other day I might have argued with him. The whale was far from our shore, and the likelihood of a shark swimming close to our beach was small, but that day I was excited to attend the birthday party, and I didn't want to get into any trouble and give my mother an excuse to make me stay home.

The winds did change, as my father had predicted, and by that afternoon, they were blowing across the moors located to our east, covering the pungent scent of the decaying whale with the pleasing odors of thistle, cow parsley, and wisteria. The balloons that had been tied to the bridge in the park bounced beneath the marbled, dusky stripes of a low, spring sky. As we approached the garden gate, we saw children of all ages. The boys from my class were chasing each other on the wide, sunny fields, and the girls were sitting demurely on the swings, watching.

"Thank you for coming to my party," the birthday girl said politely when I approached the swings and handed her the glass jar my mother and I had filled with shimmering cowrie shells. She placed it next to a tower of elaborately wrapped gifts.

She didn't look at it again.

 Kelly Jarvis

I would have preferred running wild with the boys, but I was determined not to miss any of the girls' conversations. I was already thinking about how I would mouth some secret word to them when our teacher turned her back to write our homework assignments on the board the next week, imagining the smiles that would follow as I prompted a memory the four of us shared. I listened for almost an hour as the girls gossiped, talking about the plans they had made for half term and arguing about which boy in our class was the cutest. I had little interest in either topic, so I pulled on the ropes of my swing to rock myself from side to side, using my toe to trace swirling designs in the sand beneath my feet.

My eyes drifted over to a large pile of rocks where my brother was playing a rough and tumble game with a group of older boys. Callan was faster and stronger than most boys twice his age, and even though he was young, his play was intense and competitive. He had perched himself atop the highest rock, daring the other boys to unseat him. After several failed attempts to knock him from his position, the boys had teamed up, looping around Callan as they devised a cooperative strategy. A few of them drew his attention to the front while one boy prepared to surprise him from behind. I knew the sneak attack would be a success because my brother was so busy boasting he had no idea what was coming. Still, I wasn't worried. Even if Callan lost the game, the boys would all end the day as great friends. Callan had inherited my father's magnetic personality, and everywhere we went, people loved him.

The boy behind Callan jumped up and pulled hard at his legs. My brother tumbled onto the grass as another boy from the pack scampered up the rock to claim victory. Callan wasn't hurt, and he was already laughing despite the reversal of his fortune, but he had been so surprised by the maneuver that a cry of peril had unwillingly escaped his throat as he fell backward, and my ears had pricked up at the sound. In seconds my mother had crossed the park and scooped up my brother, growling at the other boys who scattered toward the tree line in fear.

The park grew still. Everyone was looking at my mother. She called out to me, letting me know in no uncertain terms that it was time for us to go home. When I didn't move, she called for me again, louder this time, using the guttural sounds that only Callan and I understood.

My brother, who had been noisily protesting our mother's interference in his game, immediately quieted and settled against her hip in submission, but I shook my head.

I wasn't ready to leave the party, and she wasn't going to make me.

My rebellion against my mother's authority lasted only as long as it took for her expression to change from frustration to fury. When she started walking toward me, I stood up and turned to face the girls from my class.

"I have to go," I said, hoping I could make a graceful exit before my mother reached the row of swings.

"But the party isn't over," one of them replied. "We haven't even cut the cake yet."

"I know. I'm sorry." I glanced at my mother who was rapidly closing the distance between us. "I have to go."

"At least take some cake home with you." The birthday girl waved her own mother over to slice and box four pieces of the homemade confection for me to share with my family.

I shot my mother a pleading look, silently begging her not to embarrass me any further while we waited for the cake. She stopped her forward progress, but sighed with impatience.

"Thank you," I said, hurrying away once my classmate handed me the boxes. "Happy Birthday."

✳

"How was the party, Isla?" my father asked that evening. We had just finished dinner, and my mother had cleared away our plates and carried the boxes of cake to the table. She had given me the largest slice, the only one decorated with the pink sugar roses I had been so excited to try. I had refused to talk to her after she had made me leave the park, and I knew she was giving me the best slice of cake to apologize for what had happened that afternoon.

I shoveled a forkful of cake into my mouth so I didn't have to answer my father's question. The blackberry filling reminded me of the sugary medicines Dr. Sutherland used to prescribe for me when I was sick, and the pink sugar roses dissolved on my tongue, sticking between my teeth like grains of pebbled sand.

✳

My primary school held a small ceremony on the last day of our final term, wishing the leaving class farewell as we headed into break and prepared to move on to Kirkwall Grammar School, a prestigious secondary academy first established by Bishop Bjarni in 1200 AD. I was excited to go to a bigger school with students from across our archipelago. I hoped it would help me find some new friends, friends who had never heard stories about my mother and her embarrassing behavior.

At the ceremony, my teacher presented me with an award for my reading and writing skills, which far surpassed the skills of the other children in my year even though I had been late to begin my formal instruction. I hadn't told my family about the award, but when I walked across the auditorium stage to receive my gold-stamped certificate, I saw my mother sitting in the back of the room with the other mothers, holding Callan on her lap. After the presentation, our teachers instructed us to file back into our classroom and join our family members for cups of celebratory juice.

My mother handed me a bouquet of wildflowers she had gathered from the bluffs. She had tied the sea pinks, linseed, and meadow buttercups together with a long string of grass. She smiled at me, her eyes full of pride, clicking her tongue against the roof of her mouth three times in quick succession.

The girls standing next to us dissolved into giggles at the strange sound.

Kelly Jarvis

"My name is *Isla*," I hissed, when my mother leaned in to hug me.

I let her flowers drop to the floor, and she stared at me, her lips pursed tight, until I lowered my eyes, picked up the broken bouquet, and followed her out of the classroom.

Twelve

At my father's insistence, Callan began attending school the next year, just before he turned five. My brother was less thrilled with the idea of formal education than I was. He preferred to stay home and scale the western cliffs and sea stacks, bringing my mother feathers from the high-perched nests of roosting birds. He often got into trouble at school because he couldn't sit still at his desk or concentrate on his work, and as soon as the end-of-day bell released him, he would run all the way up the hill to our house, tumbling down the bluffs on the other side to let the cold ocean waters wash all traces of the classroom from his skin.

My father worked hard to contain and direct Callan's energy. Each week he took my brother fishing, teaching him to bait hooks and haul nets, activities that required patience and planning. Callan preferred to chase the fish that darted through the shallows, and my mother used to laugh when they came home from an excursion, Callan's bucket filled with more catches than my father's.

When Callan was seven, my father decided he was old enough to learn how to cast long lines into the waves and reel in the large fish that swam off-shore. The process required razor-sharp hooks strong enough to pull in the game they sought, and my father taught Callan to clean the jagged edges of the hooks before finding a steady place to stand on the rock formations cropping up from the beach.

"Take your time, Callan," my father reminded him one afternoon as my brother grabbed a used line and hook that had been discarded on the rocks. The items rested in a stagnant pool of cloudy water rich with mud and debris, but before my father could stop him, Callan had rushed headlong over the stones and swung the pole backward with all his might.

He hadn't realized my father was standing behind him.

My father threw his arms up to protect his face. The flying hook sliced into the skin and muscle of his hand, and he groaned in pain as blood welled up around the thick steel, coating both sides of the sharp, rusty barb that had thrust itself through the center of his palm.

"Wait!" he yelled, as my brother unthinkingly dropped his pole into the churning waters and hurried toward my father to help him. The receding tides bent and tossed the rod, hauling it out to sea and dragging my father, whose hand was still attached to the line, with it. He fell hard on the rocks, and the hook pulled against the weight of his body, tearing through his tendons and digging deeper into the pocket of his flesh. He fumbled as he pulled his knife from his belt and unsheathed it, cutting himself free of the line just as Callan's pole was snapped in two by the crashing waves.

"Papa!"

I couldn't keep the panic from my voice as I watched the scene unfold. I had been basking in the sun, drawing the feathered wings of a red throated diver in my journal, and my papers and pencils fell to the sand as I rose and ran toward the rocks.

We helped my father to his feet. He had been battered by the rough landscape as he slid toward the sea, and his clothes had been torn to shreds. He held his shaking hand high above the level of his heart. Blood poured steadily from the wound, staining the sleeve of his tattered jacket red.

"I'll be fine," he reassured us.

His words were calm, but his breath was shallow. He squeezed his wrist in his left fist, trying to stem the flow of his blood with the strength of his grip.

"There's nothing to worry about," he said, his voice already growing weaker.

I knew there was plenty to worry about. We had to find a way to stop the bleeding, and then we had to do something to prevent infection. My father and Callan had been fishing in brackish waters, and the gaping wound was likely filled with bacteria that could cause sickness, or even death, if left untreated. The hook would have to be stabilized and the barb cut away before we could pull it out without causing more harm. Then the layers of his flesh would need to be stitched back together. Even if we could mend the lesion, the damage that had already been done might have devastating consequences. My father worked with his hands, and the injury might prevent him from performing his duties on the

Kelly Jarvis

farms and fishing boats, bringing financial hardship to my already struggling family.

Callan and I helped my father climb over the wet rocks and walk back up to our house. I was afraid he might faint, so we sat him at the kitchen table and wrapped a towel around his hand. I sent Callan to find my mother while I went to the bathroom to gather first aid supplies. I had studied emergency medical treatment in my science classes at school, and I was reasonably certain I could perform the procedures necessary to stabilize the wound before we made the long journey to the medical center to get the help we needed.

When I returned to the kitchen with bandages, I found my mother sitting by my father's side, one hand resting on his shoulder to steady him. Her other hand, already coated with the wound's blood, gripped the visible part of the offensive fish hook, as if she meant to pull it out without first securing the barb, a careless action fraught with danger.

She looked at my father. He writhed uncomfortably, taking a deep and labored breath. I opened my mouth to tell my mother to stop, but before I could speak, my father nodded at her, almost imperceptibly, and she ripped the hook from the hollow of his hand.

The metal barb sliced through his palm, shredding his flesh like paper, and the kitchen echoed with the howling release of my father's agony.

My mother took his hand in hers, stroking the sore spot with her fingers until his breathing slowed and his shoulders relaxed. The rusty hook lay on the table in a pile of kelp and loam, its curved shape punctuating the thousand questions that were running through my mind as I tried to comprehend what had happened.

My father leaned forward to rest his brow against my mother's. He looked into her eyes. She caressed him, her movements soft and sweet. Then she lifted his injured hand to her lips, kissed the vacant space where the hook had been, and slowly, slowly, began to lick the wound clean with her tongue.

I backed out of the room before they could notice me, returning the cotton balls and antiseptic wash to the bathroom cabinet. When I closed the mirrored door, it was my mother's reflection which stared back at me, though she was still sitting at the kitchen table with my father. In that moment, I suddenly realized how much I looked like her. Now that I had grown older, our faces, two oval moons with glowing, freckle-kissed skin, were mirror images of each other. That day, I knew I would always see my mother whenever I caught sight of my own reflection, whether it was in the clear windowpanes of the shops that lined Kirkwall center or in the still pools of water left behind by the tides.

If I hadn't been so afraid of the sharp bite of the glass, I would have smashed the mirror to pieces.

My father refused to go to the medical center, letting my mother wrap his hand in fresh towels and drinking a large glass of whisky to dampen his pain. His wound healed quickly, far more quickly than my first aid books predicted, but it would be years before I could erase the phantom taste of my father's blood from trickling down the back of my throat.

Kelly Jarvis

Thirteen

The time I spent studying at Kirkwall Grammar School blurs into one long memory of endless migration. The academy was located on the opposite side of Mainland from our house on the bluffs, so while we had moved from North Ronaldsay to be closer to the Orkney schools, my daily journey to and from Kirkwall was still a long and arduous one. Each morning during school terms, I had to set out early and walk several miles to the nearest village where I could board a cross-island bus. My solitary trek through the verdant landscapes of spring and summer was a pleasant one, but when autumn drew down its evening skies, and geese began to gather in empty fields that had been harvested of their grains, my walk became tedious. The winds would whip up from the dark seas, and I would have to pull my coat tight around my chest as I leaned into the blustering gales on my way home each evening.

"Why do we have to live so far away from everything?" I asked one night at dinner after a particularly difficult day of study. I was sixteen years old and had taken a part-time job in the school library. I would collect and organize the returned books, placing them back on the shelves so new readers could find them, a task which gave me immense pleasure. When my work was finished, I would sit at my little desk among the ordered stacks and read. I felt safe in the library, circled by a wall of knowledge that separated me from the wild world beyond, and I hated leaving early to make my long trip back home.

"We aren't even close to the village center," I said when my parents ignored my complaints.

"We're close to the sea." My mother buttered a slice of bread and placed it on Callan's plate as she spoke. "That's all that matters."

"That's not *all* that matters." I pushed the dinner my mother had prepared across the table.

My father glanced over at me, his jaw tightening at the sound of my disrespectful tone, but that night I was restless, and I didn't care what he thought. I was tired of having a mother who was different from all the other mothers. It was *her* fault we had to live on the isolated, western coast of our island, and it was *her* fault I had to spend so much time traveling back and forth to school.

"Why can't I stay in the residence halls?" I asked.

The dormitories for Kirkwall Grammar School provided housing for students from the outer islands whose daily commutes would have been even longer than mine and impossible to sustain. I had several friends in my classes who lived in the residence halls. They came from the northern

Kelly Jarvis

islands like Sanday, Eday, Stronsay, and Papa Westray, and while they missed their families, they all enjoyed living with students their own age. The dormitories had common rooms with pool tables and board games, and the students often pushed aside the furniture in the dining hall to host club activities and events.

"None of your cousins live in the residence halls, Isla," my father said.

"All of my cousins live in *Kirkwall*," I countered. "And I *never* get to see them." I knew it was an exaggeration even as the words escaped my mouth. I saw my cousins regularly at school, and had become quite close with a few of them, but when we visited my grandparents' house for the holidays, my mother still made excuses for why she couldn't attend, and I didn't want to miss an opportunity to find fault in her. "Why can't we spend more time with our family?" I asked.

"*We* are your family," my mother said, taking my bait and matching the volume of her voice to mine. She thumped her chest and swept her arm through the air to indicate she was talking about the three other people sitting at the table. "And we live *here*, by the sea."

"Well, *you* can stay here by the sea, and *I* can—"

"Enough, Isla." My father's voice was quiet, but severe. I wished, for once, he would take my side instead of my mother's.

"But, Papa—"

"I said *enough*." He pushed my plate back in front of my place as I stood up to storm away from the table. "Sit down and finish your dinner."

I lowered myself back into my chair and picked up my fork. Then I moved the food around my plate, pretending to eat, until the fish and potato stew my mother had made grew cold.

*

I never brought up the topic of living in the residence halls again, but during my last year at Kirkwall Grammar School, my parents did allow me to stay at my grandparents' house on weeknights so I could attend the evening sporting events and school assemblies designed for older students. There were football games, rugby matches, and choir concerts, and as long as I returned to my grandparents' house by my curfew each night, I was given the freedom to visit my cousins and socialize with my classmates in the residence halls. Sometimes I missed the sounds and smells of the western coast, but for the most part, I was thankful I didn't have to cross the island to return home each night.

"What are you doing after graduation?" was the question of the year from aunts, uncles, and teachers. Several of the boys in my class were going into the fishing and farming industries as all the men in their families had done before them, and some of the girls were already thinking about marrying and starting families of their own. My school counselor had recommended I apply to University and further my education in cultural studies, but the older I grew, the more restless I became. I had always been academically curious, wanting to learn as much as I could about the world

 Kelly Jarvis

around me, but lately I had trouble focusing in class, and I stared out the window during lectures, my lungs burning with the far off scent of the harbor as my instructors droned on and on about history and mathematics.

Enrolling in yet another school sounded tedious, but I wasn't interested in settling down either. I had been shying away from the attention of boys since my teenage years had begun. I was quiet, and did little to attract notice. I wore my school uniform a size too big to hide my figure, and I left my hair long and loose even though shorter styles had come into fashion. Still, the boys always chased after me, and I found their attention exhausting.

"He's looking at you," my friends would say whenever we carried our trays through the lunch room.

"You're so lucky!" my cousins would croon whenever I received roses from a courting suitor.

"You'd make a splendid couple," a teacher once joked after I completed a presentation with a boy from my class. The boy had high-fived his friends as the other students burst into laughter, and I had taken my seat at the back of the room, mortified by their teasing. The teacher had later apologized for speaking out of turn, but the damage had been done, and rumors swirled about my relationship status for weeks after the presentation was finished.

When my grandmother found out the boys in my school were interested in me, she encouraged me to accept their invitations. "All love stories begin with a first date," she said, braiding my hair and tinting my lips with her make-up as she helped me to get ready for a school dance. I winced as she tugged the thick stands at the base of my neck. "You never know when you are going to meet the *one*."

I was inexperienced with dating, but I had read romance novels and been swept away by stories of young women who found their lives' purposes in the arms of noble dukes and princes. I wondered if my grandmother was right. Maybe I just needed to find the *one* to settle the restlessness that had been growing in my heart.

"Where did my parents go on their first date?" I asked. My father had only ever told me about meeting my mother on North Ronaldsay's untamed beaches, but they must have had a proper date at some point.

"Not all relationships have to be as difficult as the one your mother and father have, Isla." My grandmother tied my hair with an elastic and began pinning my braid into a coil at the back of my head. "Marry a nice boy from Kirkwall," she said. "A boy who understands the value of family tradition."

I dug my nails into my palms to stop myself from reacting to my grandmother's thinly veiled criticism about my mother being from the north. As tense as my own relationship with my mother had become, my heart swelled in defense of her whenever anyone else said something negative. No one understood the troubled push and pull of my parents' union more than I did, and I knew it was wrong of my grandmother to blame my parents' marital struggles wholly on my mother.

"Leave her alone," I heard my grandfather say when my grandmother stepped out into the hall to fetch a shawl for my shoulders. "Isla's only seventeen. She's far too young to be thinking about marriage."

Kelly Jarvis

"Marriage is *exactly* what she needs," my grandmother whispered back. "She has too much of her mother's wild spirit in her, and the sooner she settles down the better."

My father had once told me that he had pined after my mother for fourteen years before she agreed to be his wife. I wondered if she had evaded my father for so long because she had wanted something more from her life than to be a wife and mother. Maybe that was why their relationship was so turbulent. Maybe my mother was drifting helplessly on life's currents while we fed on what she had to offer, none of us considering how much she had sacrificed for our family, none of us thinking to ask her what she might need.

If my grandmother had her way, I would end up married to the first boy who proposed, whether I cared for him or not, and my own dreams would decay like rotting flesh as I stared out the window at the wide expanse of the Atlantic Ocean, remembering a life that had been stolen from me.

Fourteen

On the last day of the term, my graduating classmates and I followed a bagpiper down Kirkwall's cobblestone streets, making the traditional march past St. Magnus Cathedral. It was humbling to walk in the shadow of the ancient building, which belonged not to any church but to the people of our island, and our headmaster had told us to contemplate how we might personally contribute to Orkney's storied history as we walked past the "light in the north" to begin our adult lives.

The cathedral seemed so old that I imagined it must have been present at the dawn of our islands' creation, a sacred place where our first people had gone to worship. It had been used as a chapel where couples joined their lives in matrimony, a prison to hold women who were accused of black magic during the dark days of Orkney's witch-hunts, and a tomb for 17th century Kirkwall residents who were buried beneath its sandstone floors. Its arched windows, stone pillars, and iron scrollwork had withstood centuries

Kelly Jarvis

of buffeting from the island's wild winds, and the adjacent graveyard, whose residents were a curious mix of Nordic and Scottish cultures, dated all the way back to the middle ages.

St Magnus was a sight to behold, but as we rounded the corner and continued walking, I couldn't help glancing toward Kirkwall's coastline, where the primordial ocean, the womb of all life, heaved and rolled. She had lapped her salty tongue against the rocky shores of Orkney for eons before men had cultivated land or venerated saints, though no cathedral had ever been constructed in her honor.

That night, my classmates held a party at the community center in Kirkwall. I wore a new dress, an uncomfortable one cut of pink lace, which my grandmother had chosen. Someone started a bonfire on the lawn that sloped down toward the harbor, and as the night wore on, we all gathered there to pass around a flask of whisky, toasting the end of our school days together. I had never had alcohol before and the harsh flavor burned my throat and made my head spin.

"Let's walk down to the water's edge and get some air," a boy from my class offered when I said I was feeling dizzy. I took his hand and followed him away from the noise of the party, grateful because I didn't want to get sick in front of my friends. The sea breezes made me feel better, and we stood for a few minutes, holding hands as we listened to the waves slap against the hulls of the boats moored in the bay.

The mournful call of a foghorn pierced the quiet of the evening.

"What are you doing after graduation?" he asked, and I raised my hand to my mouth to stifle a giggle. He sounded exactly like my aunts, uncles, and teachers who had all been badgering me about my plans for the future since the beginning of the school year, and his question seemed at odds with the ephemeral feeling of the evening.

He smelled like meat and whisky, and a palpable warmth emanated from his body, settling over me and making me feel flushed. It was mid-June, the week of the summer solstice, when the sun lingered just over the horizon, refusing to sleep. The simmer dim skies sparkled with their amber light, and the stars were so faint that they looked like lost jewels buried beneath layers of gritty sand. He pulled me into a dark corner near the boat house, and I couldn't see his eyes. I was trying to remember whether they were blue, like the freshwater Loch of Harray, or brown, like the soft underbelly of a hermit crab, when I felt his fingers come to rest on the tops of my shoulders.

His thumbs stroked the lines of my collar bone. A shiver ran down my spine.

"Did I say something funny?" His voice was low and husky, and I couldn't discern whether he was amused or angered by my laughter.

I stopped giggling and shook my head, in part because I didn't want to offend him, and in part because I couldn't remember why I had been laughing. Everything seemed hazy and far away. I swallowed nervously. My mouth was dry. I wished he would offer me another sip of whisky from the flask in his jacket pocket.

He moved his fingers along the curve of my jaw and down to the cleft of my chin.

 Kelly Jarvis

"You're so beautiful, Isla," he said, tilting my face upward and kissing me until my legs trembled with longing.

I backed against the wooden slats of the boat house to steady myself, and just when I thought I might pass out from the lack of oxygen, he broke his lips away from mine and lifted his eyes to look at me. I panted, trying to fill my parched lungs with air, hoping it wouldn't be long until he kissed me again.

"You're so beautiful," he repeated, as though there was nothing else to say. He trailed his mouth across my cheek, letting his lips tease the lobe of my ear before moving down to the hollow at the base of my neck. Soon my body was burning with a strange, tingling fever, responding to the heat of his hands as they circled my chest. A cry of animal desire escaped from my throat, but then his hands became more aggressive, pawing at the buttons of my dress, tearing the fabric away from my skin. My cry of pleasure quickly turned into one of indignation.

I pushed him away.

He looked surprised and confused. Then he started to laugh, thinking my protests were part of some romantic game. He smiled as he tried to kiss me again, the way he had before, the way I had wanted him to. I bit down on his lower lip, and this time, he was the one who whimpered.

"Ow!" He took a step back from me, gingerly wiping the blood from the corner of his mouth. "What's wrong with you?" he demanded

I didn't respond, but my eyes flashed, and he held up both hands in a conciliatory gesture. Then he returned to the party, leaving me all alone.

My breath was still coming fast and thick. My hands were shaking, though I wasn't sure why. I had wanted him to kiss me. I had liked the way his hunger had made me feel, but when he had tried to remove my dress, when he had torn the lace as though the fabric was his to destroy, everything had changed.

I didn't blame him for being upset with me. He hadn't hurt me, not really, and he had stopped touching me as soon as I protested, but he had broken several of the buttons on the front of my dress, leaving my undergarments exposed. I couldn't go back to the party, and I couldn't go back to my grandparents' house. My grandmother would find a way to blame *me* for what had happened, calling me a wild thing, saying I was the one at fault, even though I had only pushed him and bitten him to make him stop.

I ran toward the harbor, following the blinking lights of the bouncing boats. I ran until the wooden docks that lined the civilized bay gave way to stony lanes. I ran until I passed the outskirts of Kirkwall, where the splashing waves of the North Sea churned.

I kicked off my shoes and walked along the shallows. The ocean waters were cloudy with silt. My feet sank into the earth, leaving a trail of footprints in the dampened sand. When I glanced backward to see how far I had come, the waters that pushed against the shore had erased the marks of my journey. When I glanced forward, there was nothing but smooth, flat ground as far as the eye could see.

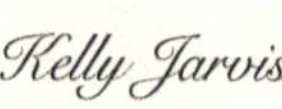

 Kelly Jarvis

"Where have you been?"

My father greeted me with equal parts anger and relief as I walked into our house the following day. When he saw that my dress was torn, his face clouded over with concern. "Isla, are you alright? Did someone hurt you?"

I shook my head and then nodded, answering his questions out of order.

"I'm fine," I said, though my head was pounding from the whisky I had drunk the night before.

At the sound of my voice, my mother rushed into the room. She pulled her knitted shawl from her shoulders, wrapping it around mine to cover me. She ran her hands over the length of my body, inhaling my scent to search for injuries.

"Where have you been?" my father asked again, the second iteration of his question more aggressive than the first. "Your grandparents expected you to come home last night."

I twisted my mother's shawl in my fingers. The wool was soft and warm.

"Your mother and I have been looking for you for hours. We thought something happened to you."

"I'm sorry," I said, even though I wasn't.

"Where have you been, Isla?"

I knew he was only angry because I had worried him, but I didn't want to talk about where I had been. What had happened at the party seemed insignificant compared to the way it had made me feel. *What's wrong with you*, the boy had asked me, his voice laced with disgust. His words had upset me because I knew there was truth beneath them. Something *was* wrong with me. I had felt a restlessness growing inside me ever since we first left the shores of North Ronaldsay. I had done everything I could think of to stave it off, drowning myself in my studies and blaming my mother because I didn't fit in on Mainland. Now, for the better part of a year, I had spent my weeknights in Kirkwall, away from my mother, and still, I couldn't shake the feeling that I was incomplete. I didn't know what I wanted from my life, and I was afraid I would never find the place where I belonged.

My mother looked from my face to my father's. Then she shook her head to quiet him.

"She's been out all night," he said, surprised by my mother's uncharacteristic defense of me. "She could've been hurt."

My mother shook her head again, steering me down the hall to my bedroom. I was worried she was going to interrogate me too, but she helped me out of my torn dress and washed the remnants of my grandmother's makeup from my face. Then she sat down on the bed next to me, taking my hand in hers.

I wanted to tell her all the things I was feeling, but we had lost the closeness we had shared when I was a child, and even then, words had never been our way.

She traced the outline of my hand with the pad of her thumb, pausing briefly at the vacancy between each of my fingers. I remembered the way she used to hold Callan's hands up the light to kiss his delicate webbing when he was small. The sun would filter through the translucent layers of his infant skin, making his beautiful webs glow like little golden halos. In my studies, I had learned that this kind of

     Kelly Jarvis

webbing, called syndactyly, is caused by a genetic mutation not uncommon in our part of the world, but when I was a little girl, I had simply believed, like my mother, that Callan's webbing was a miracle. Now, for the first time in my life, I wondered if I had been born with webbing like my brother. I wondered if my father had asked Dr. Sutherland to cut it away. I wondered if it was possible to forget the violent removal of the flesh that makes a person whole.

I fell into a deep sleep that afternoon, waking in the middle of the night after everyone else had gone to bed. My room was bathed in the golden light of the simmer dim, and I noticed that the drawer of my old wooden nightstand was slightly ajar. When I was younger, my nightstand was the place where my mother had left me gifts from the sea, broken shells and frosted glass made more beautiful by the ocean's wild caress. The tiny treasures had been her coded way of sharing her world with me, her way of telling me a story without using words. I thought I had outgrown our childhood ritual, but something beyond reason prompted me to pull open the drawer.

Inside, I found a key.

Fifteen

The key was large and heavy. It was made of iron, and the ancient scrolls of its bow and barrel were patinated by time. I held it in my hands, feeling the cold metal against my fingers. Then I tiptoed down the hallway and pulled my father's sea chest from its resting place in the bottom of the closet. I hadn't seen it since that night so many years ago when my father had tried to set it on fire, and I ran my finger over the top right corner where its wood was still scarred black from the flames. Despite the damage my father had done, the chest was impenetrable, impossible to open without the corresponding key. Its contents had always been kept hidden from me when I was a child. Now, I knew my mother wanted me to see what she had shrouded beneath its watertight panels.

I could have opened the chest right there in the house, but instead, I dragged it outside, down the bluffs to the foot of the tumultuous Atlantic, a fitting place to unlock my mother's secrets. My pilgrimage took me well over an hour. The sea chest was stubborn and difficult to move, and it often stuck between the rocks. I pulled and tugged, denting its corners and jostling its mysterious contents. Three times I wanted to turn back, thinking it would be easier to crawl under my covers and pretend I had never found my mother's gift in the drawer of my nightstand, but I had found it, and the key had loosened something inside me. My curiosity was too strong an instinct for me to let it go.

The rocks eventually gave way to dunes, and the rope handles of the sea chest wrote blisters onto my palms as I struggled to pull its weight through thick grass and wet sand. When I finally reached the shoreline, I dropped to my knees in exhaustion. I looked over my shoulder, my eyes following the long, smooth trail left behind by the chest. It wended all the way back to our little house on the bluffs, which was quiet and dark in the simmer dim light. Marsh orchids and red campion bloomed across the front lawn, their petals fluttering like swarms of monarch butterflies that had perched on branches to rest in the middle of their migratory journey.

The sun still burned, hot and gold above the horizon, plunging its rays into the blue sea and streaking the air above with shades of violet and periwinkle. The clouds blowing in from the north were soaked with rain, and their droplets blended the muted tones of the air and ocean like watercolor paints. It was well past midnight. Morning scavenger birds were already patrolling the shoreline, their calls joining the cacophony of wind and waves churning over the rocks.

I took a deep breath and slid the key into the lock. The pointed teeth and hollow grooves clicked against each other as they latched into place, a perfect fit.

The steel hinges of the sea chest, which had not been opened for decades, creaked when I lifted the lid. A waft of musty odor mingled with the salt air, and behind it was the briny scent of my mother's skin. I reached into the chest and pulled out a sealskin dress, its leather still soft and supple. I unfurled it across my lap in wonder, running my hands over its velvet warmth and bringing its folds to my face. My lifetime of loneliness, my endless struggle to fit in, could be explained by the pelt I held in my hands, if only I opened myself to the miracle of it. My mother was a selkie. It was her blood, feral and free, that flowed through my veins.

In every selkie story I had ever heard, selkie women returned to the sea, leaving their human husbands and half-human children behind. If it was true that my family's story was a part of selkie lore, then the chronicle of our tale was an unexpected discovery, like an elusive cowrie shell found shimmering beneath a starlit sky. My mother had not left us, even though she must have been haunted by the savage call of the sea. My father had not pushed her away, even though it would have been far easier for him to marry a nice girl from Kirkwall who understood the value of his family traditions. And Callan and I had not been abandoned, even though we had been born and raised on the turbulent coast where nature wages her endless war against man's hostile advances. Our family's story was proof that the love which unites us is far stronger than the fear which threatens to tear us apart.

Kelly Jarvis

When I was a little girl, my father told me that he had locked my mother's seal coat up tight and hidden the key so that she could never leave us, but the key inside my nightstand, which had been gifted to me by my mother, told a more nuanced story. My father may have stored my mother's pelt in his locked sea chest, but my mother had always had access to the key that would open it. She may have been a wild creature, but she was not my father's prisoner. She had chosen to love him, though they came from different worlds. She had chosen to stay with him, though her primal heart had suffered at the hands of his flawed humanity. She had chosen the three of us, her family, again and again, though it required a willing sacrifice of her undomesticated soul.

My mother had given me the key to my father's sea chest because she wanted me to understand that choosing to love another begins with first knowing and loving ourselves. For seventeen years I had known only half of my ancestral legacy. Now my mother was gifting me the chance to discover the truth of her past so that one day, I would have the wisdom I needed to choose my own future.

The sodden clouds blew in from the north, coating the rocky shore in diaphanous dew. I stood up and removed my clothes. Raindrops fell over my naked body, glistening like tears of joy. I stepped into my mother's sea dress. The fur, mottled like the face of the moon, scratched and chaffed as it slid over my curves, but soon it clung to my chest and hips, downy and light, a second skin.

I dove into the spiraling surf, salt sealing the edges of my miraculous transformation. I heard the far-off keening of a family I had never known, and I headed out for deep, dark waters, trails of silver fish lighting my way. The solstice sun, knowing he must soon yield his light to our island's long, winter nights, trembled in the skies as I frolicked through the waves, a free and glorious wild thing.

❅

My only daughter was born beneath a full moon sky streaked with far-off lightning. She arrived late in my life, long after I had returned to North Ronaldsay, the island where my parents' romance, the prologue to my own story, had begun. Callan's wife had already given birth to several sons, tall, strapping boys who lived in Kirkwall and doted on their infant cousin as though she had slid down from heaven. My parents had already passed away, their ashes mixed together and scattered into the swirling seas.

When my contractions began, I charted their strength and frequency, carefully calculating how much time I had before I would need to leave my little house on the western shore and report to the medical center. I had traveled the northern regions of the world before meeting my husband at University, where we had both earned degrees in cultural studies, anthropology, and marine science, and we had both agreed that the safest way for our child to enter the world was under the care of educated doctors and nurses. But, as my womb began its incessant throbbing, I shook my head against our careful plans. My husband narrowed his eyes to

Kelly Jarvis

express his hesitations. Then, when I insisted, he followed me outside into the crisp, autumn night.

We made our way to a large saltwater pond, created when our island's governing council constructed a breachway connecting a freshwater channel to the open ocean. The full moon hung like a silver shield in the sapphire sky, and her reflection shimmered, round and bright, in the still, dark waters below.

My husband wrapped his arms around me as I lowered my cramping body into the cold water. It wasn't until I began to writhe in increasing discomfort that he pleaded with me to reconsider my choice.

"Please, Isla," he said, "let me take you to the medical center." He stroked my wet, tangled hair. "You don't have to do this alone."

"I'm not alone," I said, refusing to leave the water. I squeezed his hand as another contraction twisted through my abdomen. I was grateful he was with me, but I also knew that on the far side of the salt pond, floating by the tall grasses so they wouldn't be seen, was a group of female grey seals. They had adapted to the confluence of fresh and salt water created by the breachway, and they came up the channel to birth their pups and teach their young to hunt minnows in the shallows of the protected pond. When I began to moan with the pain and effort of pushing, the seals swam slowly back and forth, their deliberate movements creating soothing ripples that lapped against my rigid womb.

At the height of my agony, I cried out for my mother, bringing my tongue to the roof of my mouth and letting it fall over and over to create the sound of my infant call. Lightning flashed as my baby crowned and slipped from body. I reached down to lift her from the salt water's embrace, cradling her so she could nurse. Her tongue clicked against the swell of my breast, three times in quick succession. The winds and waters beyond the breachway began to howl and rush as I stared into the eyes of my newborn daughter. They were stormy and grey, the color of a winter afternoon, and between each of her fingers and toes was a translucent web of gossamer skin, as thin as paper.

"She's beautiful," my husband said, kissing her downy, white fur.

"Her name is Morgan," I whispered, "after the seas that circle our island home."

"Morgan," my husband repeated, the letters liquid in his mouth. "Our daughter."

When Morgan had taken her fill of my milk, we bathed her skin in the magic beams shining up from the water and down the sky, and the grey seals gathered in the darkness around us, singing their wild songs of longing and love to the light of the Selkie Moon.

✳

By the time Morgan had arrived on this earth, I had long since forgiven my father for what he had done to my mother and to Callan. I knew he had only sought to cut away the pieces of my brother that others would never understand, but although there were many on North Ronaldsay who whispered in hushed tones about Morgan's peculiar webbing, my husband and I refused to allow anyone to defile the natural condition of our daughter's exquisite hands.

Morgan learned to love what others called her malformity. Her webbed hands and feet helped her swim through rough, ocean waters and grip the rocky outcrops along the western beaches where she chased after our island's feral sheep as her uncle had before her. Morgan's webbing receded as she grew, and by the time we had celebrated her seventh birthday, the gossamer threads connecting her fingers and toes had all but disappeared. I held her hands in mine that night, tracing the empty spaces between her fingers with the pad of my thumb, like a stargazer searching for earth shine to prove the crescent moon is still whole.

"Do you know what a selkie is, Morgan?" I ask my daughter each night as I tuck her beneath her covers. At only eight, she is already too old to believe in faerie legends about selkie brides, but her eyes light up at my question because she knows it is the way I preface all my stories about the sea. Morgan loves to hear about the Finfolk, ocean sorcerers who sail from Orkney to Norway with only seven powerful strokes of their oars, and she can already recite *The Grey Selkie of Sule Skerry* from memory, but her favorite sea stories have always been the ones I tell her about my own adventures beneath the waves. Tonight, I speak of the lonely whale songs that circle through the deep like eddies and the indigo shadows that slip beneath moonlit skies. I tell her about my father's sea chest and my mother's iron key. I describe the soft leather of the sealskin dress that fit me like a glove. She sits up against her pillows, animated by my tales, wanting to ask me a thousand questions about the northern regions I have traversed, and a thousand more about the grandparents she has never known, but bedtime has come, and I will hear none of them.

Each time I tell Morgan the story of the night I used my mother's key to open my father's sea chest, she only half-believes it true, but on storm swept days when the tide is high, she turns my words over and over in her mind until they shimmer like shards of sea glass worn smooth by the pounding surf, promising her that one day, she, too, will have the power to choose.

Some say stories are simple things, washing up on the shores of bedtime to carry children off to sleep. Some say stories are fragile things, delicate webs that can be easily cut and scattered across the coasts of time like forgotten memories. But stories are also powerful things, their broken fragments collected by scavengers who roam the wild banks of life and love searching for the truths that bind us all.

In the stories my father used to tell, I was sent from heaven and my brother came from the sea. This was his way of teaching us that we are both children of Orkney. Born on the lands where the North Sea kisses the Atlantic, we are the keepers of selkie legends, the heirs to sacred tales that blur the borders between animal body and human heart, between savage and civilized, between feral and tame. Though we may sometimes lose ourselves in the darkness of our northern winter nights, we will always find ourselves again in the light

Kelly Jarvis

of our stories, which we gather like treasures from the seas that endlessly roll and writhe beneath our storm-soaked and miraculous skies.

Author's Note

first learned about selkies at The Carterhaugh School for Folklore and the Fantastic, a virtual institution run by folklorists Dr. Sara Cleto and Dr. Brittany Warman. I was enrolled in a class titled *The Wine-Dark Sea: Folklore of the Ocean*, and the brilliant Terri Windling joined us to deliver a guest lecture on selkies, the seal people who live in the cold ocean waters surrounding Scandinavia, Ireland, and the Northern British Isles. Windling spoke of selkies as hybrid creatures, shapeshifters who discard their seal skins to sing and dance in human form. My favorite fairy tale, *Beauty and the Beast*, plays with the construct of animal and human hybridity, and my favorite place, the seashore, pairs the wild ocean with the civilized land, so it was no surprise that after learning about the seal people's liminal existence, selkie stories began swimming through my reading lists and floating on the currents of my imagination.

Like all folklore, selkie tales and their meanings change over time, morphing into new shapes as different cultures, generations, and artists add unique brushstrokes to the

Kelly Jarvis

legends' landscapes. Although stories of seal people can be found all over the world, the selkie stories that I studied came from the islands north of Ireland and Scotland, the Nordic shores, and the coasts of Iceland and Nova Scotia, places where seal populations flourish. Seals also swim off the New England beaches where I spend my summers, and I vividly remember the day I saw a seal, her pelt chocolate brown against the blue hue of the sky, as she darted through the waves while I played in the Atlantic with my oldest son. She disappeared as quickly as she came, but her fleeting presence sent a chill down my spine and left me wondering about the mysterious creatures who make their home in ocean waters.

Traditional selkie legends tell of fishermen who fall in love with beautiful selkie women, stealing their seal coats to trap them on shore. These tales echo with loss and sadness, themes often unavoidable in stories about the sea. A human cannot survive in the ocean, and a selkie cannot be content on land, so any romantic encounter between the two requires emotional risk. Early selkie tales about unions between the species were often used to explain peculiar family traits like syndactyly, a genetic condition that manifests as a webbing between the fingers and toes. Selkie stories also helped people explore the ever-evolving relationship between civilization and nature, a relationship that has always been fraught with anxiety.

Selkies fit into the folkloric tradition of stories about animal brides and grooms, but while selkie men are often cast as seducers who romance human women with their toned physique and animal charm, selkie women are often presented as prey, condemned to a domestic life on dry land by the violent removal of their animal skin. In their human forms, selkie women fall in love with their partners, raising children and finding happiness, but, when they discover their hidden skins, usually with the help of their growing children, they almost always return to the sea, leaving their human family behind. Unlike the beasts of fairy tales who transform into princes, selkies remain wild creatures at heart, and when given the choice, it is the call of the sea, and not the call of domesticity, that they heed.

When I first decided to write a selkie story, I wanted to explore the idea of choice at the heart of the legend, presenting a marriage between a selkie and a fisherman whose love for each other was imperfect but true. My fisherman would not deny his beloved selkie her full freedom, and my selkie, given the opportunity to return to her wild home, would decide to stay with him, accepting the transformations, both painful and miraculous, that accompany her difficult choice. The happily-ever-after of my selkie and human union is not the stuff of fairy tales; it is a happily-ever-after spun of both joy and grief because it recognizes the powers and limitations that define mortal life and love.

Since legends, the category of folklore that selkie stories most often fall into, are usually linked to specific places, I searched the northern oceans for the perfect spot to set my tale. It was Orkney, an enchanting archipelago situated between Scotland and Shetland, which called out to me. Orkney is steeped in selkie folklore, and when I read about North Ronaldsay's drystone dyke, a barrier constructed to

Kelly Jarvis

divide the cultivated farmlands of the island's interior from the feral, seaweed-eating sheep roaming the wild shores, I knew I had settled upon the perfect place for a story about the tumultuous union between nature and civilization.

I have never been to Orkney, but its haunting liminality speaks to me. In my research, I learned that, traditionally, Orkney citizens were both fishermen and farmers who came from both Nordic and Scottish backgrounds. The islands' topography features both gentle, flat beaches and wild, rocky coastlines. The medieval St Magnus Cathedral, located in Kirkwall, Mainland, one of the oldest and northernmost cathedrals in Britain, features carvings of both humans and animals in its sandstone steeple. And, each year during the holiday season, the residents of Kirkwall take part in a Ba' with two teams competing to move a ball between an inland goal and a watery harbor. The beautiful islands, rich with stories of trows, fairies, selkies, and Finfolk, are both contemporary and primal, and the more I studied Orkney's history and culture, the more I fell in love with it. I knew the story I wanted to tell belonged on Orkney's shores.

Writing, for me, has always been a process of discovery, and as my selkie story set on Orkney was beginning to take its shape, I was most surprised that it was the voice of the selkie's daughter which kept coming through. In traditional selkie tales, it is often the selkie's daughter who reveals the secret location of the stolen seal coat, losing her mother to the call of the ocean before she understands the weight of what she has done. I began to wonder what it would feel like to be the child of a union of opposites, to know that your mother has a secret life beyond her ordered family role, a life that calls out to her in equal measure to the call of her romantic and maternal duties. As I started writing, I realized that although few of us can claim selkie heritage, we are all children of these complex unions. We all use our human minds and animal bodies to come to terms with our place in this world. We all have mothers whose lives stretch beyond the confines of their family roles, though we rarely stop to think about our mothers as women who harbor hopes and dreams that may be at odds with the life choices they have made. Filtering my story through the voice of the selkie's daughter allowed me to flush out the complicated roles women play within conventional family structures. By reversing the trajectory of traditional selkie tales and giving a selkie mother the power to reveal the secret location of her own seal pelt to her daughter, *Selkie Moon* advocates that we all cherish our untamed skins, even if we choose not to wear them.

Although selkies are understood as hybrid creatures that are part animal and part human, some legends posit selkies as fallen angels who plunged into the sea when they were expelled from heaven during Lucifer's fall. These narratives link lowly selkie stories to sacred myths which explore the intersection of the animal, human, and divine. This genealogical ambiguity further classifies the selkie as an "other," and countless artists have explored the selkies' otherness in a myriad of interesting ways. Some have used selkie brides to represent cultural otherness, gendered otherness, or sexual otherness, interrogating and propelling messages about marginalized populations and queer identities, while some have used

Kelly Jarvis

selkie brides to explore the "other" within the self. We are all selkies of a sort, wearing different skins as we navigate the world, discarding pelts to hide from persecution and donning dresses to unleash our truest forms. As a woman, wife, mother, writer, poet, professor, daughter, and friend, I have slipped in and out of many skins in my lifetime. Some have been worn threadbare by use, while others have hung in the back of my closet, patiently waiting to be unfurled. My writer's pelt was pushed aside while my husband and I built our home and raised our young children, but it has always been a part of who I am, and stepping into it, even as it chaffed and scratched my skin, helped me to discover my voice and tell my story.

In *Selkie Moon*, Isla's mother and father are storytellers as well. Her father uses words to craft his tales, while her mother creates coded messages with objects she gathers from the shore, the liminal place where the wild ocean waters meet the cultivated earth. It is only by integrating the stories that both of her parents tell her that Isla comes to understand her personal and cultural history, an understanding she passes onto her own daughter by telling stories in turn. At its heart, *Selkie Moon*, like everything I have ever written, is about the sacred act of storytelling itself, a humble pastime that wields the highest magic. Through the gossamer web of stories, our pasts are connected to our futures, and both our animal instincts and human desires are woven into the tapestry of the divine.

My deepest gratitude goes out to Kate Wolford, the Founder and Editor Emeritus of *The Fairy Tale Magazine*, my mentor and my friend. Without Kate, I would never have unlocked the sea chest that guarded my writer's skin or released my story to swim free in the tumultuous seas of publication. I am also thankful to Kristen Baum DeBeasi, Editor-in-Chief at *The Fairy Tale Magazine* and Lissa Sloan, author of the Cinderella continuation *Glass and Feathers*, for all of their help and advice. My thanks go out to the award-winning historical fantasy author Juliet Marillier who kindly shared her knowledge and love of Orkney with me, Holly Dunn, the artist who designed my cover which features the glowing beauty of the Selkie Moon, a symbol of transformation, and Alison Weber, the artist who created a stunning selkie illustration for all of my early readers at *The Fairy Tale Magazine*. I am also grateful to the friends and students who have joined me to play in the realms of fairy tale and folklore. Most of all, I am forever grateful to my husband and our three sons, who have watched from the shores while I tapped away on my computer, riding the waves of joy and grief that swell over the ocean of storytelling. Randy, Keegan, Reilly, and Kasey, you are my greatest treasures and my most precious gifts. I would choose you every time.

A writer's list of gratitude is incomplete if it does not acknowledge her readers, and this is especially true for writers who work with folklore, a tradition that springs from the folk rather than from the mind of an individual creator. I am eternally grateful to the keepers of selkie legends who have come before me, and I am eternally grateful to the readers who will breathe new life into the selkie tale I have set down. Storytelling is a collaborative act, its migration completed

 Kelly Jarvis

only in the minds of the audience, its purpose revealed only in the liminal space between the teller and the listener. In this way, the gleam of even the smallest story can be refracted into a thousand shades of light that shimmer on the horizons of endless skies. I can never thank you enough, dear reader, for adding your magic to my words. I am humbled to have met you on the shoreline of *Selkie Moon* and I hope, one day, our paths will cross again.

Kelly Jarvis works as a Contributing Writer for *The Fairy Tale Magazine* and teaches writing and literature at Central Connecticut State University. Her poetry and fiction have appeared in *A Moon of One's Own*, *Baseball Bard*, *Blue Heron Review*, *Corvid Queen*, *Eternal Haunted Summer*, *Forget Me Not Press*, *Mermaids Monthly*, *The Chamber Magazine*, and *The Magic of Us*. Her Cinderella retelling, "A Story of Soil and Stardust," published in the World Weaver Press anthology Mothers of Enchantment: *New Tales of Fairy Godmothers*, was nominated for a Pushcart Prize. *Selkie Moon* is her debut novella.

Visit Kelly online at kellyjarviswriter.com.

Kelly Jarvis